MAKING MARCO

MARCO'S MMA BOYS
BOOK 7
BY
S.M. DONALDSON

Table of Contents

˜S.M. DONALDSON˜

<u>Making Marco</u>

Copyright © 2019 SM Donaldson

Cover by: Indie Vention-Designs

Cover Model: Lance Jones

Photography by: RLS Photography

Editing by: Chelly Peeler *Ink It Out Editing*

Proofreader: Kimberly Holm

Beta Reader/Comment Bubbler/ Ride or Die:

E-Book Version

ISBN-13: 978-0-9983100-5-3

Print Version

ISBN-13: 978-0-9983-100-6-0

INTRODUCTION

- ***Intended for mature audiences only 18+***

- This book is written in a true southern dialect, from a true southern person. Therefore, it is NOT going to have proper grammar. That being said, the "g" isn't cut off of every "ing" ending.

DEDICATION

To my fans who've stuck with this series from the beginning. A series I wasn't even sure about when I started it, I really didn't know how it would do. But you guys loved it and I can't tell you how much I appreciate that.

DESCRIPTION

If you love something let it go...it's not that easy.

Vance DeMarco and Elaine Storm have a history. Once full of love, passion, and pain.

Time has torn them apart and yet, brought them back together. This time with families, businesses, and tons of responsibilities, too.

Their story is truly about life's second chances.

Because as the saying goes, when it comes back...it's simply meant to be. Except nothing in love is ever simple.

NOTE FROM THE AUTHOR

Dear Reader,

I'm happy to bring you this final chapter in the Marco's MMA Boys series. This book goes all the way back to the beginning of Elaine and Marco, so we'll see them build through the years. They will make you laugh, cry and get pissed off. Once you get to part three you're going to see it start overlapping with the other books. It may seem like I skim over them, but I don't want to kill you with redundancy of the other books. I really hope you enjoy this. It has been a long process and parts of it have killed me. I don't know if it's because it's the last in this series, kind of the end of an era, or if it was just that taxing to write. You can ask Chelsea Camaron, several times I wanted to throw in the towel with this book. Overall, though, I'm excited for you to get to meet teenage Elaine and Marco, getting to see where they started and how they began. Who knew their story would be so intense? It was also fun to visit the eighties and nineties, times without cell phones, texting and instant access to everything. I really do hope you enjoy this.

Now, I know what you're asking… What's next?

Well, I have one more book in my young adult series and then I will be jumping back on the spin-off from this series. Dispatch 247 1st Responder, Second Chance Romance. Once again, thank you so much for your patience and understanding. I love you all!

Love,

S.M. Donaldson

PROLOGUE

MARCO

I watched her.

For too long I simply watched her.

I loved her.

I loved her more than anything.

I lost her.

Then I found her again.

I never planned to let her go, not ever.

That's the thing about life, though, it doesn't always go as planned. The woman I love is still the girl I loved from high school. Our journey to be together went on for over twenty years and our life together has been full of kids and grandkids.

If this is where it ends, then it's been one hell of a ride.

PART 1

CHAPTER 1

ELAINE

1987

I watch him, I watch him all the time like some freaking stalker. This is insanity.

What's he doing to make me watch him this much? Nothing.

Standing at the other end of the hall leaning back against a locker with one foot propped up like it's the most casual thing in the world. He's comfortable.

Vance DeMarco is an enigma. He's that bad boy your mama warns you about. With his long black hair unruly, the cigarette poked behind his ear, jeans with a hole in the knee and a Van Halen t-shirt. But, he's everything I can't walk away from.

So simple yet so complicated in my brain. We've always been friends. He's never pushed for more so neither have I.

A cloud of Aqua Net interrupts my thoughts. I fight back the cough from choking on the perfumed hairspray. "Elaine, are you listening to me?"

Looking at my friend Brandi, I shake my head. "Sorry, I was thinking."

"Yeah, thinking about that hot piece of ass down the hall. I keep telling you he likes you, but you just won't jump for it. Hell, Melissa practically threw her birth control pills on his desk the other day to let him know she was open for business," she says, whispering dramatically.

In my personal opinion, birth control gets a bad rap. Just because a girl takes it doesn't mean that she sleeps with everyone. It just means that she's prepared if she decides to, or maybe for a medical reason. They are looking into more uses for it every day. If Melissa wants to flaunt her business to the world, well, that's on her. Birth control isn't an open invitation to have sex. Besides, Brandi is the last person who should be talking about being open for business. She's slept with more than one or two guys herself. She calls me an uptight virgin, but I think more of myself than to have sex with a guy who won't call me the next day. "Anyway, a bunch of us are going down to the river tonight to celebrate the beginning of spring break. Are you coming?"

I shrug my shoulders as I catch my breath. "Um, I don't know. I've got a bunch of stuff I need to do for that project Mr. Kimble is asking for as soon as we get back," I answer truthfully.

She puts her hand on her hip. "Look, Miss Class President, sits in the front row and never misses a day of school. We have exactly five weeks of school left when we get back from spring break. That's only five weeks left of our high school career. You need to have more fun and I'd bet my entire case of hair spray that you have most of that damn project done." Her blue eye shadow dances as she talks. "Now, I have my mom's Vette tonight and we're going out." By Vette she means her mom's Chevette, not to be mistaken for a Corvette, because Brandi's not got it like that and neither do I.

I slam my locker after I get my Trapper Keeper, "Fine. What time are we leaving?"

"I don't know yet. I'll slip a note in your locker before seventh period and let you know," she says, turning to walk away.

I quickly shuffle off to my next class. Vance actually meets me at the door and holds it open for me. "After you, beautiful."

Beautiful. I give him a smile while the butterflies do summersaults in my belly. "Thanks."

"Hey, you going to the river tonight?" he says in a low voice.

"That's what Brandi was just talking to me about. I guess. I mean, I don't have anything else going on," I say, studying the square tiles on the floor.

He gives me that sexy smirk and jerks his chin up. "Great. I'll see you there."

I quickly take my seat so the butterflies will stop in my stomach and settle.

~*~

Standing in front of my mirror putting the finishing touches on my hair, I sing along with the radio. *"Take my hand, we'll make it I swear. Whoooa livin' on a prayer."*

"Elaine! Brandi's here!" my mom yells from the living room.

Grabbing my purse, I turn off my radio and go to the living room where Brandi is waiting on me. "You girls be careful tonight. Elaine, be home before your dad gets off shift!"

"Yes, Mom!" I call out. My dad is a cop. He gets off around three in the morning. I'm a good kid so my mom is never hard on me about curfew, she knows I'll be home probably way earlier than that. Actually, a lot of times she's the one telling me not to take life so seriously. I just want to graduate and go to nursing school, so yes, I take life pretty seriously. I'd go to medical school and become a doctor, but I just don't see being able to make that happen. Cops don't make a lot of money and my mom only works part-time for a local lawyer, so there isn't a huge cash flow to send me through years of school. Plus, I want to have a family someday and not after ten more years of school.

"Girl, we're going to have a fucking blast tonight," Brandi says, getting into the car.

I shake my head. "Yeah, okay."

She bangs on the steering wheel, "No, I'm on a mission and you, my friend, will be having fun tonight." We drive through the night singing to The Bangles.

As we pull down to the river, there is a line of cars showing the party is already in full swing. "Holy shit, there's a lot of people here! How is the law not going to get called? I swear to god, Brandi, if my dad gets called down here to bust this up and I'm here, I'll be grounded for the rest of my life."

She shakes her head as she pulls down her denim skirt. "It's supposed to be a big party, duh! The cops do get called every once in a while, but for the most part they leave us alone." She grabs a cigarette from her pack and lights it. "I swear, sometimes I forget that you're such a homebody." She walks ahead again and then spins around. "How are we friends?" Sometimes I wonder that myself, but I don't tell her that.

"Because I gave you part of my peanut butter sandwich in kindergarten," I reply like a smartass. I always do since she's been my best friend forever.

She laughs like she always does. "That's right, bitch. Now, let's go get you some beer, or at least a wine cooler."

We make our rounds talking with friends, or well, more Brandi flirting with the available guys. I'm on my second beer when I walk up on him propped up against one of the guy's trucks. He tips his chin up and smiles. "Lainey girl, you made it." His friend next to him tugs Brandi over by the wrist and she falls against him giggling.

I give him a small wave. "Yeah," I point to Brandi, "she really didn't give me much of a choice."

He pushes off the truck, walking toward me, "Well, I'm glad she didn't." He pulls the cigarette from behind his ear and lights it. "Let's go for a walk." He reaches in a cooler and grabs two more beers.

I glance back to my friend and she motions for me to go. With anticipation pushing me on, I walk down a beaten path with him. "You ready for this beer?"

I finish the last few swallows of mine. "Yeah, sure."

"So," he drags out. "High school is almost over."

He seems almost as nervous as me which is hilarious considering he's Vance DeMarco. "Yep. Almost finished."

He takes a drag off of his cigarette. "You still planning on nursing school?"

I don't know how he knows that. "Yeah." I guess the way I drag it out clues him in.

He exhales a small cloud of smoke. "You told me once when we had Chemistry together."

"Oh, wow. I can't believe you remember that." I really wasn't aware he'd ever paid that much attention to what I said.

One side of his mouth draws up into a smirk. "I like to know things about you."

I try to hide the blush rising in my face. "So, what about you? What are your big plans?"

He clears his throat a little. "I've already signed my enlistment papers for the Marines," he explains, dropping his cigarette.

Something drops in the pit of my stomach. "Wow."

He nods. "Yeah, tell me about it." I'm still processing all of this. "I catch the bus three days after graduation for Parris Island."

I take a big swallow out of my beer, causing it to go down the wrong pipe and I spit part of it out. He steps over, grabbing my arm. "Are you okay?"

I clear my throat and try to laugh it off. "Yeah."

He brushes a stray piece of hair away from my mouth. "Maybe try not to chug the beer."

"Maybe not," I say in a whisper.

He clears his throat. "You know, I've always thought about you." He places his hands on the sides of my face. "I've wanted to do this for a long time. I hope you don't mind." Before I can reply, his lips are on mine.

I drop my beer and wrap my arms around his neck, kissing him back. He tastes like a mixture of mint, cigarettes and beer. My body tingles. I've been kissed before, but never like this. Honestly, my first kiss was Michael Kestoner and it was disgusting. The boy slobbered so much I had to wipe my mouth off. Then the few guys I've kissed since have been better, but still nothing touches this. His lips are soft, he leads, he guides, he takes, and I give. His hands slide down my sides, landing on my ass. "Mmm," he moans against my mouth, pulling away a little. "That's everything I thought it would be."

I swallow hard. "You've thought about it?" I question, my heart thumping in my chest.

His hands rub the globes of my ass. "More than I care to admit."

"How come you never said anything?" I whisper, our faces still close enough to touch.

"Honestly, I didn't think I deserved you." His voice is deep but strained. I want to ask why he would think he didn't deserve me, but I don't want to ruin this moment. I don't want him to retreat.

I open my mouth to say something but before I can, someone yells, "Yo, Vance! You out here?"

He steps back, releasing me. "Yeah!" he calls out. "Be there in a sec!"

I look around nervously and turn to walk back to the party. He tugs at my wrist. "Hey, what are you doing tomorrow night?"

I shrug. "I don't know."

"Come out with me. I want to spend some more time with you. Pick you up at six?" I'm not really sure if this is a question or a demand, but I'm so turned on I can't think straight.

"Uh, um yeah, sure," I bumble through my response.

He briefly kisses my lips again. "Good."

After he walks away, I wonder if he even knows where I live. I'm not even sure he has my number, but I'm not that desperate girl who is going to call out after him.

I follow his lead up the trail and find another beer, while in search of my best friend. She's still hugged up to one of his friends when I find her. She raises her eyebrows when I walk up, I tip my head to the side letting her know I'm not talking in front of that guy.

She whispers something into the guy's ear and he smirks as she walks away, following me away from everyone.

Her eyes light up when we stop. "So! Tell me!"

"We kissed, and I guess we have a date tomorrow night," I answer, not sounding sure of myself.

"Holy shit, girl. You don't mess around, do you? He's all Matt Dillon in *Little Darlings,* or maybe Matt Dillon in *The Outsiders* sexy." She makes a show of shivering. My best friend totally has the hots for Matt Dillon.

I laugh, "I was thinking more Patrick Swayze."

Her eyes light up. "Oooh yeah, that, too."

I motion over to where she was before. "So, what's up with you and his friend?"

"He's just like, cool." She shrugs.

"Are you interested in him?"

Her face looks crazy. "Ugh, gag me with a spoon, no. You know I'm not settling for this place. I am so outta here when we graduate. Now you, on the other hand, will stay here and have a house and a white picket fence with lots of babies."

I laugh, "Really, that's your thoughts?"

She grins. "Yep, now before you do that, let's go mingle some more because this party is totally bitchin', you've just missed most of it making out in the woods."

Oh, but that time in the woods was everything I dreamed of.

CHAPTER 2

MARCO

Stupid, that's the only excuse I can come up with. I have done my best to stay away from Elaine all year and now just weeks before I ship out, I fucking ask her out on a date. I am an idiot. I am a damn idiot. An idiot who is thinking with his dick or his heart, I'm not sure which one. Because it's damn sure not my brain. She wants the whole domestic life and I need to see the world. If I stay here, I'm going to end up in jail or worse.

I know what people say when they see me. They think I'm a piece of trash. They look at the parents I have, my clothes, hair and cigarettes, and assume I'm going to rob them or get their daughter pregnant and ditch her.

Don't get me wrong, I've done some dumb shit. I've partied hard, banged babes, raced cars and motorcycles. Anything to get that adrenaline rush. That's one of the reasons I'm going into the Marines. I need a new rush and I'll get to see the world. I'm not made to stay in this town. I'm not okay with the judgments found here.

Now, here I am about to walk up with my hair tied back, in jeans without holes and a nice shirt tucked in, on the front porch of the only girl who could ever make me give it all up. She has no idea how beautiful she is. Call me selfish but I want these last few weeks with her. The cop car sitting in the driveway makes me realize exactly how stupid I really am. Knocking on the light blue door, I hear shuffling as someone comes to answer it. Her dad swings open the door. "Can I help you?" His voice is gruff and unforgiving.

"I'm here to pick up Elaine," I say, looking him in the eye.

His chin dips and his eyes study me. "Really?" He studies me again. "Didn't I see you the other week when I busted up that group of kids in the parking lot of the movies?"

Honesty—it's always been my policy even if it's going to bite me in the ass. "I'm sure you did, sir. As you know, there isn't much to do around here without going into Gainesville. Most of us aren't allowed to do that, so hanging out in parking lots is what we do."

His face is impassive and I'm not sure what else to say. I can't read him. "Hmm. Honesty. That's a refreshing change for a young man your age. Come on inside. I still hear that god-awful music blaring from her room, so she's probably still getting ready." He steps to the side so I can come in.

"Thank you," I say, stepping inside of the small, brick ranch-style home. Their house isn't like mine, it's an actual home. The light brown paneled walls are covered in pictures of Elaine growing up. It's neat, but not unlived in. You can tell the people here love each other. The place just has this warm feeling that certainly won't be found at my house.

He motions to the olive green couch, "Have a seat. Brandi was here a little bit ago, that probably put her behind." He laughs.

I nod. "Yes, that's a possibility."

Her mom comes in the room. "Well, hello, Vance. Would you like something to drink?" It's crazy that her mom still remembers me from all of the times she came to class parties and school events over the years.

"No, ma'am, I'm fine," I say with a smile.

"Okay, well I'll go make sure Elaine knows you're here," she tells me, walking down the hall.

"So, are you excited about graduation?" her father asks from his brown recliner.

"Yes, sir," I answer with knots in my stomach.

"What are your plans? You have started making them, right?" Her father's voice is still as gruff as it was at the door but a little more relaxed. I can tell, though, he doesn't bullshit.

I give him a firm nod. "Yes, sir, I leave for the Marines three days after graduation," I explain.

He nods his head, giving me an approving glance. "Good plans. Good career with the opportunity to see the world."

Instinctively, I roll my shoulders back with pride. "That was my plan. I'm not really the college type, not much else going on around here and I'd like to see new places." I hope I don't sound like an ass. I won't lie, he's an intimidating son of a bitch.

He nods again, understanding. "Your parents are the DeMarco's down on Bluff Street, right?"

I look to the floor. My parents aren't anything to brag about. My dad works at a local plant and drinks at the shitty corner bar at night. My mom works at the grocery store and gets pissed and shows her ass in the same shitty corner bar. I'm sure he's been called to deal with them numerous times. "Yes, sir."

He sits forward in his chair a little, looking me in the eyes. "Son, I'm going to give you a piece of advice. Don't let where you come from affect where you're going. You've got a plan, I see determination in your eyes. You're more than your past."

Before I can respond, Elaine comes out of her room in a pinstriped jean skirt and a fringed t-shirt. "Hey, sorry to keep you waiting."

I stand up and reach to shake her dad's hand. "Thanks for the talk, Mr. Loxley."

He nods, sitting back in his chair. "Keep what I said in mind and good luck in the Corps. Make sure we get your address for boot camp. I'm sure the Mrs. would love to send you some homemade goods. She used to send them to me all the time when I was in."

I nod, walking toward the door, "Thanks."

So Elaine's dad is a former Marine. Once we're out to my car, she smiles. "Sorry if my dad was a little overbearing."

I shake my head. "No, he was actually pretty cool."

She looks at me skeptically, "My father, cool?"

"Yeah, I mean I wouldn't say he was totally rad or anything, but he was just cool." I look over my shoulder to back out of her driveway. "Didn't know he used to be in the Corps." I shift my car into first gear before pulling away from her house.

"Yeah, he and my mom were high school sweethearts. He went into the Marines, they wrote letters and all of that, but she wouldn't marry him until he was out and came back home," she explains.

"Why?" I question.

"She said this was her home and she wasn't traipsing around the world. So, she stayed here and worked. When he finished his sixth year, he said he'd had enough and didn't reenlist. He was ready to come home to her."

Glancing at her, I smile, "Hmm. I guess I can see his reasoning."

She gives me a small smile. "So where are we off to?"

I shrug, "You wanna see a movie? Or we can hit up the Game Room, grab some pizza. I just wanna hang out with you," I say in complete honesty.

"Pizza sounds good, I'm hungry." She blushes a little, "And I'd like to hang out with you, too."

We sit in silence on the way to the pizza place, only the sound of Toto singing "Africa" coming from the radio. After we pull into the parking lot, it actually looks pretty empty and relief washes over me. Not that I'm embarrassed to be seen with her or anything, quite the opposite, I don't want to have to share my time with her. I only have a limited amount of time to be with her and I don't want to waste any of it with high school bullshit.

After we're seated, she looks around, "It's pretty dead in here tonight. It's kind of nice."

I grin. "Yeah, it is." I point to the jukebox along the wall. "You wanna play some music?"

She nods, and I hand her some quarters. "Go ahead, I'll place our order. Anything you don't like?"

"Onions, anchovies and hot peppers are my only no-go items."

I tip my chin up. "Okay then." I watch her bounce over to the jukebox and start looking through the selections.

The waitress stops by our table and I order us some pizza and Cokes. Elaine comes back over to our table and I motion to the tabletop Pacman game. "Wanna play?"

She grins. "Are you any good?"

I tip my head back, laughing, "Psshh. You act like you don't know me."

She laughs at me. "You're on, DeMarco."

Her laugh is truly the best thing I've ever heard. We start playing the game and trash talk the entire time until our pizza arrives. The waitress gives me a flirty look as she sits it down but I don't give her the slightest hint of attention.

After we've finished eating, we walk out to my car and I open her door for her. "So, where to now?" I ask.

She smiles, sitting down in the car. "Anywhere. I'm like you, I just wanna hang out."

I grin, gently closing her door before walking around to my side. "Okay, so you wanna just drive around?"

"Maybe, or is there somewhere we can just go to talk?"

I nod. "Yeah, I know a place."

I drive us down by the same river we were at the other night, but I go past where we were and stop at a small boathouse and dock. I shut the car off and grab my flashlight as we get out. She looks around as I point the light forward. "Wow, this place is pretty neat."

"Yeah, I come down here when I want to be alone." Really, it's when my parents are at each other's throats and I don't want to listen to it anymore. Only, I don't share all of that with Elaine. This time with her is too special to drag it down with the bullshit that is my parents.

"It seems like it would be a peaceful place to think."

I nod, placing a hand on the small of her back to guide her down to the dock. "It is."

There is enough moonlight that I can see her smiling at the end of the dock looking over the water. "Wow, it's just beautiful." She sighs.

I swallow hard, watching her. *Yeah, she is.*

CHAPTER 3

ELAINE

Sitting at the end of this dock talking with him feels like the most natural thing I've ever done. I've always known Vance is smart but talking with him relaxed like this, I can see he is a thinker. His thoughts are too big for this small town. I can totally see him traveling the world and making a difference. "You really are beautiful, Lainey," he says out of nowhere.

I giggle a little. "Thanks."

"I mean it," he replies, brushing his hand over the side of my face.

"What did you mean the other night when you said you didn't think you deserved me?" I ask because I haven't been able to get it out of my head.

He brings his other hand to my face, looking into my eyes. "I meant that some guy from the trailer park with shitty parents, the guy with nothing to offer, doesn't deserve you."

"Vance, you're more than that. Don't ever think of yourself as less than, because you're so much more." How can he think these things about himself? Being bold, or bold for me, I raise myself up a little so my face is level with his and kiss him on the lips lightly.

That's all it takes for him to pull me in tighter. "Holy shit," he moans as I slide my arms around his neck. "I could easily get addicted to you, Lainey."

"What's stopping you?" I whisper, just before he slams his mouth back to mine.

He reaches under my ass, picking me up as my legs wrap around him, straddling his lap. "Wow," I say as we break the kiss. I feel the air on the back of my thighs where my skirt is now bunched just under my ass.

He rests his forehead against mine. "Fuck, Lainey. I need to stay away from you, but I can't. I need you to be mine until I leave."

"What about after that?" I ask.

"I'll never ask you to wait around for me. You deserve all of the happiness in life you should have, but all I'm asking for is this little piece of time." His voice is almost shaking.

I tug the rubber band he has pulling his hair back out and run my fingers in it. "You've got it."

Our mouths collide again, hungrily starving for each other. I feel my nipples tightening under my thin bra as his hands slide up my sides. My pulse is racing. I want him to touch me. *Touch all of me.*

"Oh, I intend to," he replies, making me realize I said that out loud. He pulls my shirt over my head, leaning in to kiss the tops of my boobs.

My heart thumps inside of my chest and I feel the need to squeeze my thighs together. I grab the bottom of his shirt and pull it off, then run my hands down his cut chest. He goes right back to kissing my chest and neck. "Oh god," I moan out.

He takes that as the go ahead to unclasp the front of my bra and his mouth goes directly to the nipples that are hard enough to cut glass at the moment. He rolls us over so that I am beneath him.

My hands glide down to his jeans, rubbing his hard cock through the rough fabric. Something takes me over and I want to touch him. I've never wanted anything like this before. I nervously try to get the button of his jeans undone when he pulls back a little. "We don't have to…"

I stop him. "I know, but I want to touch you."

He gives me a small nod before helping me unbutton and unzip his jeans. I reach my hand inside of his underwear, grasping his thick cock. He lets out a loud groan as I start to stroke him. His mouth goes back to licking and sucking on my nipples as one of his hands travel down my stomach and under my skirt. His fingers find the wetness between my thighs and as he starts moving them, I cry out. My hand moves faster on his cock.

The more he gives, the more I want to take. Removing my hand out of his pants, I reach down, attempting to shove my panties down. He pulls away, making me panic momentarily before I realize he's removing them for me. When Brandi told me to wear the cute red panties I had, I seriously thought she was an idiot, but I'm damn glad I did now.

He spreads my legs wider, rubbing his thumb over the bundle of nerves between my folds. Staring into the night sky, I cry out. I feel him move and next his tongue moves to the spot where his thumb was. "OH, Vance!"

It's not long before my body feels like it's going to explode, and I scream out to God and anyone else who hears me. He sits up with a cocky grin before lying back down beside me, pulling me tight against him. I try to catch my breath, "That was intense."

He smirks, "Yes, it was." He kisses me again and I can taste myself on him. Which stirs up more feelings, making me feel hot again. I can feel him still hard against my bare thigh. I have an idea so I push him onto his back and start kissing down his chest, tugging at his jeans and underwear until they're further down. This is the first time I've ever seen a cock except for in videos. I've heard my friends talk about giving blow jobs and how they think it's gross, but I'm not feeling that way right now. I lean forward, taking him in my mouth. I hear him groan and his hand goes to my hair, gently guiding me as I suck his cock. Soon, I feel his body tense and warm liquid spills into my mouth.

After I pull away and swallow, he pulls me back up beside him, kissing me hard. Brushing my hair away from my face, he says, "Lainey, I've never felt anything like that before."

I giggle, "Me either."

He presses the button on the side of his watch, making it light up. "I hate it, but I have to get you home."

I stand up slowly, pushing my skirt back down from around my waist, then grab my bra and slip it back on, along with my shirt. I glance around the dock, looking for my panties as he is zipping his pants. "Where are my panties?"

He shakes his head. "I don't know."

I cover my face. "Oh my god, they're probably in the water. They must've fallen off the dock."

He tugs my hand. "It'll be okay. It isn't like your mom sews your name in them or anything."

I let out a small laugh, "I guess you're right."

He pulls me a little. "Come on, let's get you home."

~*~

"Oh my god! He did what for you?" Brandi's eyes are as big as saucers.

I nod, holding my pillow tight to my chest as I giggle. "Yes, and holy crap did it feel incredible."

Brandi is sitting on the other end of my bed in awe. "So, you both went down on each other? Wow. Most guys expect to get theirs but not to go down and take care of business for you. Damn, girl, you scored big time."

"I know. It felt so dirty but so right at the same time."

"Wait until you actually have sex," she says with a small laugh.

"If it makes me feel like that I may become an addict."

"So what are you guys now?" She talks animatedly with her hands. "Like, was this a one-time deal or are we planning on you leaving with him when he leaves?"

I shrug, "I really don't know. We kind of both agreed that we want what we have right now. So we're hanging out, I guess, until he leaves for the Marines, then..." I can't finish the sentence. Already I'm too attached and the thought of not having Vance is like a vice around my heart.

She leans back against the wall. "Wow." Then she smirks, "I'm kind of proud of you. See, I told you the dirty girl panties would work."

I toss the pillow I'm holding at her head.

She catches it and smiles. "I just hope you can handle it when he leaves."

I sigh and flop back on my bed. *Me, too.*

CHAPTER 4

MARCO

I look around at the cheesy decorations the gym is covered in and laugh at myself. I never thought I'd be caught dead in a damn tux with a hot pink cummerbund and ruffled shirt, standing in the middle of a crepe paper-filled gym, but here I am, and I'm damn near ecstatic about it. All because I'm here with the greatest girl in the world.

She's in a hot pink sequined dress with nothing holding those great tits in but a ruffley shoulder strap. Oh yes, those are great tits. In the past few weeks they've been in my hands and in my mouth.

Trust me, I've screwed around with girls before, but with her it's another thing. After the night at the dock, I can't seem to keep my hands off of her and she seems to be the same with me. My little class president can be a minx. We've fooled around any chance we get. In my car, in the library, under the bleachers in the gym, and one night I even got brave enough to sneak in her window. The farthest we've gotten is some hot third-base action. I guess the best part to me is knowing that besides kissing, I own all of her firsts. She and I plan to take one more of her firsts tonight. Normally, I would never plan so much ahead just to have sex with a chick, but with her she deserves the best. So I went to a small motel in the next town and reserved us a room. I'm not taking her virginity in the back seat of my car or on a damn dock. It's going to be in a bed like she deserves.

I watch her out there dancing with her best friend and see how happy she is. It almost makes me sick to my stomach, because I have to leave her in two weeks. She's promised to write me while I'm gone, but I've told her not to wait on me. I can't stand the thought of her not living the life she's always dreamed of because she fell in love with some jarhead who's out roaming the world, that jarhead being me.

I smile as I see her walking toward me. "Hey, they're about to do the garter dance, are you ready?"

I give her a smirk. "For me to run my hands up your leg in public? You're damn right I am," I lean in close to her ear, "but you can bet that probably after that we're gonna need to go. My hand can't get that close to the heaven between your legs without needing to touch it."

I hear her breath catch and she shivers. "Okay."

I pull back a little and look her in the eyes. "If you're nervous about tonight, we don't have to."

She shakes her head. "No, I want to."

I kiss her hard as the DJ calls for us to come to the dance floor. Once "Take My Breathe Away" starts playing, I walk over to her and go down on my knee, reaching under her dress, and run my hands over her smooth legs, sliding the garter down.

Standing back up, I slide the garter up my arm like the rest of the guys and pull her close to dance with me.

"I'm ready to go, Vance." It comes out breathy and needy. Thank fuck!

As soon as the song ends, we make our way to the door, practically running to my car. My dick is so hard and these pants do nothing to hide it. It feels like it's taking forever to make it the fifteen minutes to the motel. She reaches over with her hand and rubs me through the pants.

"Babe, if you keep doing that we won't have anything left to work with when we get to the room."

She giggles and sits back. I fly into the motel parking lot, jumping out and opening her door. Shoving the key into the lock on the motel room door, we burst in. She kicks off her heels and jumps to me, shoving my jacket off. My hands reach around the back of her dress, looking for a zipper. I tug it down and push her back a little so I can watch the dress fall to the floor. She steps out of it, only wearing a pair of tiny black panties and a black strapless bra.

I kick off the stupid dress shoes I have on, with the socks, and undo the cummerbund. I undo a few of the top buttons on the damn ruffled shirt before I pull it over my head, quickly shoving the dress pants down. I stand there in a pair of boxer shorts with my dick pitching a huge tent. I watch her reach around her back and release her bra, and those glorious tits. I back her up to the bed, kissing her neck and shoulder like I know she likes. I push her back on the bed and lean down to remove her panties, seeing the patch of dark brown curls between her thighs. Leaning forward, I kiss the inside of her leg all the way down to her slick wet center.

She squirms and cries out as I lick and suck on her clit. "Vance, please, now. I want you now," she pants out.

Standing up, I grab a rubber from the stash I put in the nightstand when I checked in earlier. Shoving my boxers down, I roll the rubber down my throbbing dick and lean forward over her. Kissing her mouth hard, she squirms with anticipation against me. Reaching between us, I line the head of my cock up with her entrance. I pull back from her lips, "I care a lot about you, Lainey. You know that, right?"

She nods, "Yes."

I slowly push into her, letting her get used to me as I go until I hit the resistance. This is a first for me, too. I've never been with a virgin before. "Keep going," she moans out.

I pump back a little before I bust through that barrier, sinking inside of her completely as she cries out.

I stop. "Are you okay?"

She nods, "Yes. I just need a second." She takes a deep breath, "Okay, I'm ready."

It's a good thing, too, because I'm about to explode. She's so fucking tight and it feels great. I start pumping into her. I want this to be good for her so I reach down and rub her clit as I move. I can finally see that she's relaxed and enjoying it. She moves against me as she moans. "Oh god, Vance."

I feel her pussy tighten on my cock and I don't know how many more pumps I give before I shoot everything I've got into the condom. I brush the hair back from her face. "Wow, you're perfect."

She shakes her head. "No, I'm not."

"Close enough for me," I say before getting up to dispose of the rubber. I see the evidence of her innocence on it so I go into the bathroom and get a warm wash cloth to help her clean up.

Looking at her lying in that motel bed, I shake my head. I'll never be what she needs. I want everything she has to give, but I just can't take it from her. No, I was right in the beginning, she deserves the man who wants the kids and the house. Not a life moving from base to base waiting for me when I'm stuck on a boat or in some damn port with no way to communicate.

I feel a burn in the pit of my stomach when she looks over and smiles at me. I just don't know how in the hell I'm going to do the right thing when I have to leave here.

CHAPTER 5

ELAINE

Getting out of the shower, I hear the phone ringing, followed by my mom saying, "Just a minute, I'll check. Elaine, phone!"

Grabbing my bathrobe and throwing my hair up in a towel, I run out of the bathroom to the kitchen and grab the phone. "Hello."

His deep voice rumbles through the phone line. "Hey."

I start walking down the hallway with the long phone cord for privacy and sit down. "Hey," I say with a smile.

"Are you busy tonight?"

"No, I have to eat supper with my parents, but that will be done by like six," I answer back.

"You wanna go see a movie? The theater still has that new Michael J. Fox movie, or *Beverly Hills Cop II* just came out."

I smile. "Well, Brandi drug me to see Michael J. Fox as soon as it opened so, the new *Beverly Hills* movie is fine."

"Sounds good. Do you need to check with your parents before we say it's a go?" he asks.

"No, I don't give them much to worry about so they don't give me a real hard time about going out."

"All right, movie starts at seven, so I'll pick you up about six-thirty?" he asks.

I smile. "I'll see you then."

"Oh and Lainey."

"Yeah?"

"Wear a skirt."

I giggle, "Maybe," before I get up to hang up the phone.

My mom startles me. "So, big plans with Vance tonight?"

"Yes. Well, after I eat supper with you guys. He's gonna pick me up around six-thirty. We're gonna go see that new *Beverly Hills Cop* movie," I answer as I start walking down the hallway to my room.

She follows me to the door of my room. "Honey, I like Vance, he's a nice guy, but I just don't want you to get hurt when he has to leave in two weeks."

I nod, "I know it's coming, we've talked a little bit about it. I plan to write him while he's gone and if it's meant to be, it's meant to be. If not, we'll have enjoyed ourselves these last few weeks of school."

Mom nods even though I can tell she doesn't believe me. "Okay. Well, you go ahead and get ready then. Be home by midnight."

"Yes, ma'am," I reply as I start pulling out my clothes.

~*~

Right on time, there is a knock at my front door. I apply one last coat of lip gloss before I run out of my room to the front door. My mom is already talking to Vance in the living room. "Hey," I say as I walk in, "sorry, I was just finishing up."

"I was just telling Vance that your dad and I want to invite him to dinner one night before he leaves," she says, smiling brightly. I know they want to do this because they feel like his parents aren't going to do anything for him.

"Yeah, we should do that," I say with a smile.

He nods. "Thanks, Mrs. Loxley, I don't want you guys to go through any trouble just for me."

She pats his arm, smiling like a proud mom. "No trouble at all. I enjoy it, and I think Hugh wants a chance to reminisce."

My mom gives him a huge glowing smile. "Great, we'll get it planned. Make sure you give Elaine a list of your favorite foods."

We both nod before I practically push him out the door. "We're gonna be late for the movie if we don't go now."

"You two have fun!" my mom calls out.

After we're in his car, he grins at me and runs his hand over my bare leg. "I see you wore the skirt like I asked."

I blush and push his hand back a little. "Yes, but don't think you're going to make me miss the movie, bud."

He shakes his head, smirking. "Okay, I'll wait until after the movie then."

~*~

I promised myself I wouldn't get attached. Now, I can barely look at this food we're fixing for him tonight because he's leaving in two days and all I want to do is cry.

"Thanks again for inviting me over to eat, Mr. Loxley, I don't get a nice grilled steak that often." Vance brought me back to what I was working on.

"Not a problem, son, I love a good excuse to use my new barbeque pit." My dad wasn't kidding with that. He'd pretty much driven my mom crazy last fall building this brick monstrosity in our back yard.

I finish bringing out the pan of baked beans we've done while Mom brings out the corn on the cob to our enclosed patio

"So, Vance, do you have all of the essentials you'll need before you leave?" This coming from my mom, always worried about people needing things.

"I'm going to go to Woolworth later today and pick up a few more things. You know they only let you bring certain stuff, so I don't need a lot," he replies, holding a platter for my dad to place the steaks on.

"Make sure you get some foot powder when they let you go to the exchange. You're gonna need it in your boots. Well, if they'll let you have it. Sometimes they won't," my father says, taking the last steak off of the grill.

"Will do," Vance replies.

"You been doing any conditioning?"

I wanted to answer that for him, *oh yeah, he's conditioned all right.*

"Yes, sir, been running five or six times a week, sit-ups, push-ups and swimming every chance I get."

"You decide about your car? You gonna leave it with your folks or sell it?"

He'd worked and saved for that car, I really hope he doesn't leave it with his useless parents.

"I was gonna see if you knew someone who would help me sell it and if you could just hold on to the money for me." It amazes me how quickly he's formed this bond with my dad.

"Sure thing, son, or I'll tell you what, we were thinking about getting Elaine a car for college. Would you be interested in selling it to me?"

Vance nods. "Yeah, we can talk more about it in a little bit."

Once everything is on the table and we're seated, Dad says our blessing and we start to eat. That feeling shows back up in my stomach again. He's going to leave and I'm going to be sitting around here waiting. Looking at the steak, baked beans and corn on my plate, I have no appetite. The smell of it all is making me pure nauseous.

"Elaine, did you hear me?" My dad's voice interrupts my pity party.

I glance up from my plate. "I'm sorry, no."

"I asked if you'd gotten all of your paperwork filled out at the college yet?"

"Oh, yes, sir. I'm all set to get started in a couple of weeks."

Vance looks at me. "I thought you'd start in the fall."

"I could, but I want to be on rotation to start the nursing program by a certain time without taking a break. So, I'm going to start knocking out some prerequisites soon."

"Oh, well that sounds good."

"Now, Vance, don't you worry, I've already talked to Hugh and when you graduate, we're coming up there."

"You guys don't have to do that," he answers.

"No, I've wanted to go back up there since I graduated from there myself," my dad replies to him.

Has anyone even considered me here? How hard it'll be for me to go see him and leave him again? Then it hits me what a selfish bitch I'm being, because from what I know his parents could give two shits about him. This is his future and what he wants to do. I can't be a distraction.

"Will you be able to come with your school schedule?" he turns, asking me.

"Um, I'm sure I'll be able to work something out," I say, quickly looking back at my plate, hoping no one notices my heart breaking.

Thinking back to what he's said to me, it hurts. *"Elaine, it's not fair for me to ask you to wait on me, but damnit if it isn't harder than I expected for me not to ask you to wait."* He brushes my arm with his hand up and down as we lie at the end of the dock. *"I can't ever imagine finding another you."* I mean we originally agreed to enjoy each other right now, however, it's like we have this pull to each other I can't explain.

So far our options are, a) see how the long-distance thing goes, b) me go with him as soon as I can or c) call it quits and let it go.

I glance up at him again as he's talking to my dad and realize, I'm not sure if I'll ever be able to completely let him go.

CHAPTER 6

MARCO

Fucking torture, that's what this is. Seeing the tears roll down her face. I use my thumb to brush them away. "Hey, you'll be my phone call, okay? I'll let you know I'm there and as soon as I can, I'll get a letter to you."

She sniffs, "You can't use your phone call on me, you need to call your parents."

I motion around me. "Do you see them here? Do you think they're worried about me? No, you're here, you own me. You've gotta know that by now, Lainey."

"Load up!" our driver calls.

I give her one last kiss before pulling away and taking the first step into the rest of my life.

I find one of the few empty seats and as I sit down, I look at her out the window as she watches me. "Hey, you mind if I sit down here?"

I look up to see a guy close to my age, kinda like me, hard around the edges. "Yeah, sure."

He slides into the seat and sticks out his hand. "John Beck, nice to meet you."

"Vance DeMarco, same here."

"You from around here?"

"Yeah, I'm local," I answer.

"I live about thirty minutes from here. That your girl that was standing outside with you?" he asks. Man, I hope this guy isn't the super chatty type.

I think about his question. "Yeah, I guess she is," I say with a smile.

He grabs a magazine from his bag and opens it up to start reading. I lean my head against the window and try to drown out the sounds of the road as we barrel down the interstate headed to my new life.

~*~

It's funny how fast the weeks can fly by. Fifteen weeks ago, I made that first phone call to Elaine and since then we've written letters as often as possible. I get to see her tomorrow at my graduation. Then I get to spend a week with her before returning for more training. She's kept me posted in letters about school, she's finished her first round of classes. I knew she would, though, she's one of the smartest people I know.

I did send my parents one letter since I've been here, but not shockingly, I haven't received one back. According to Hugh, they are still alive and still causing problems in town.

John drops down on my bunk. "Hey, man, so your girl is coming up tomorrow, huh?"

"Yep. Her and her parents. Then I'm riding home with them for leave. Are you sure you don't want a ride back with us?"

He shakes his head before standing back up. "Nah, I'm gonna hang around here, nothing back there for me. You gonna tell her about your plan and the possibility of selection?"

I flop my head back on my pillow with my arm behind me. "Yeah, I have to."

As luck would have it, after meeting John on the bus here, we ended up being battle buddies. He's a great guy, a little talkative, but he comes from the same kind of family as me. Where I plan to be a lifer in the Corps, he plans to get some college money and go to school to be a doctor or some shit. He slaps my leg, "Okay, well, we'll talk more tomorrow before you leave."

I give him a small salute before settling in for the night. I don't get much rest, though. I think about Elaine and how I can't wait to get my hands on her, how I can't wait to hold her. Then I imagine breaking her heart when I tell her that I'm thinking of trying to go to sniper school after I go through Infantry Training Battalion. Which entails more missions, more time away from her if I get in and make it through it. My first duty could be in bum fuck nowhere and I just can't ask her to come with me or wait, but I don't want to let her go either.

I continue to toss and turn all night, trying to get some sleep. I know the Gunny's wakeup call will come super early.

Twenty-four hours later, I'm in a car headed back home with Elaine snuggled close to me and my balls killing me because I'm so ready to be buried inside of her.

She and her parents were the first people I saw once the ceremony was over with. Her mom had a huge bag full of homemade treats. There was even some for John. Elaine knew he and I had become friends and that he was from around home. Hugh tried to talk him into riding back with us, but John was still against it.

The hours click by on I-95 as Hugh drives through the night. He has to be back for work tomorrow. He normally works nights, but he has to testify in a court case so this was pretty much a turnaround trip for them. I tried to talk them out of it because I felt really bad about putting them out like this but Hugh insisted.

I doze off until I feel the car stop. I open my eyes to see we're in her parents' front yard. I sit up and rub my eyes. Her dad speaks first. "You can crash in the spare room tonight since we're getting back so late," her dad offers. "Go over and check on your parents tomorrow. If they start shit, Vance, leave, do not get yourself in trouble while you're on leave. You come back here and you can stay in the spare room."

I nod, climbing out of the back seat. "Thanks, Mr. Loxley."

He slaps my shoulder. "No problem. I'm heading to bed, I hate dealing with damn lawyers and judges," he growls, heading inside.

I grab my duffle bag out of the trunk before walking in the front door with Elaine following me. "I'm gonna grab a shower and enjoy not being surrounded by other men for a few minutes, if that's okay?" I say to her.

She laughs, "Yeah, I'll make sure your room has everything that you need."

I spend probably thirty minutes in the shower. It feels so great to have hot water running over me and not be limited on time and not have other men in my space while I wash my junk. Speaking of junk, getting to jack off is great, too.

Walking into the room with my towel wrapped around my waist, I finish drying and grab a pair of boxers, slipping them on. Turning out the light, I find my way over to the double bed and fall down on it. Man, this feels like heaven compared to that little twin-size bunk I've been sleeping on.

I'm just about to doze off when I hear the door come open and lightly close. I feel her body weight on the bed before she says anything. I whisper, "What are you doing sneaking in here? Your dad finds out you're in here and he'll bury me."

She kisses my neck. "They're snoring away, I checked before I came in here. I just needed some alone time with you."

I can feel my cock getting hard again already. "Babe, you're killing me here. I haven't touched you in almost four months, my balls are killing me, and my dick is already hard enough to pound nails."

I hear something crinkle. "Well, then it's a good thing I brought this with me." I feel her hand pulling my erect cock from the boxers I'm wearing. She rolls the condom on. "We have to be super quiet."

I roll, pinning her below me, "I hope we can handle that."

I reach down to make sure she's wet enough for me to enter and find her soaked. "Hmm. Someone has been thinking naughty thoughts about me."

"I was thinking about you while you were in the shower. How your muscles probably looked with soap running all over them." Her words are breathy and quiet.

I line my cock up and slide into her. I have to stop myself for a second, but she wiggles under me. "Babe, you have to stop, or this will be over in a second."

She places her mouth on mine, kissing me slowly as I can finally start to move. I know I'm going to be quick, so I reach down with my thumb and rub the little bundle of nerves between her legs. She starts to move against me and I slip in and out of her quickly. It doesn't take long before she's moaning into my shoulder and shuddering. I make two more hard thrusts and spill everything into the condom.

"Wow," she says quietly. "I've wanted to do that since I saw you in those dress blues. Well, really what I had in mind was a little wilder and louder, but same end result."

"We've got some time for that. We'll get a room one night while I'm here and you can be as loud as you want."

She smiles. "Okay."

"You better get back to your room, before we fall asleep."

"Yeah, you're right. That wouldn't be a good wake up call, huh?"

"Nope." I give her one last kiss before she goes back to her room.

Once the door shuts, I need to figure out how to get rid of this condom. I reach over on the nightstand grabbing the box of tissues, putting the condom in several of them so it's not likely to come out and toss it in the small trash can. I'll make sure I empty it tomorrow. Lying back down, I close my eyes and wait for the sun to peek through the window.

The sun doesn't get much of an opportunity to shine before I'm awake. I guess those early mornings are something you become accustomed to. I find her parents standing in the kitchen when I go down the hall. "Good morning," her mom says, smiling. "Did you get a good night's sleep?"

"Yes, ma'am, can I get a cup of that coffee?"

"Sure thing," she says, moving to the cupboard to grab a mug.

"So, what time are you planning to go over to your parents'?" Hugh asks.

"I don't know. Probably later. Last time I knew, they were both on day shift so they're probably working."

"I don't know that your mom is working at the Piggly Wiggly anymore. I haven't seen her there the past few times I've been in," Mrs. Loxley says.

I shrug. "Oh, well, maybe I'll go by earlier today." I don't really want to go over there, but I'm not going to tell them that.

Hugh hands me a set of keys. "I'll be using my department car today, so you can use my truck. I know Elaine has something at the college later."

I take the keys from him. "Thanks." I look at both of them. "I really appreciate all you guys have done for me."

Mrs. Loxley hugs me. "No problem, honey, we're glad to do it."

A couple of hours later, I'm dressed and heading down to the shitty part of town I grew up in. As I pull in front of the trailer, I see the garbage piled up on the porch, beer cans and liquor bottles spilling out of it. I shake my head and really think about turning around to leave before I even go inside.

Instead, I get out of the truck and make my way onto the porch, knocking on the door. I hear grumbling and movement inside before the door swings open and my mom stands in it. "Well, look who decided to show up."

"I just got in last night from boot camp. I have a few days' leave, I wanted to come by and check on things," I say as she backs up and lets me in.

I look around and see more of the same mess that's on the porch. "Dad at work?"

"Yeah. That asshole manager down at the Piggly Wiggly fired me, saying I came in drunk."

"Well, did you?" I ask before I can think to just keep my mouth shut.

She puts her finger in my face. "You listen here, you little shit. You think you're some damn hot shot now that you went off and left here? You ain't nothin', you'll never be anything more than what you are, trailer trash, just in a different place." She throws herself down in the recliner, lighting up a cigarette. "Yeah, we got your damn letter. I know that damn cop's family has been taking care of you, though. He stopped by to check on us and update us on how you were doing since you were sending his slut daughter letters. *Told us how great and wonderful you were, such a good boy and we should be proud.* Didn't figure you'd want shit from us anyway."

I swallow hard. Yep, this was a mistake. "It would've been nice to at least get a note back. You guys are my parents."

She lets out a huff. "Whatever. You want me to send you a letter that says shit's the same here except I got fired and your daddy is on his last warning at his job? Fuck you, Vance." She jumps up. "You're the same lowlife you were when you left here, just in better shape."

I stand up, "This was a mistake. I just wanted to check on you guys, but I can see I should've left well enough alone." Walking toward the door, I hear her laughing.

"Yep, keep walking, you piece of shit, when you fuck up and get something blown off, don't expect to come back here and me take care of your ass."

I laugh, "Yeah, I'd never expect that from you since you didn't do it in the first place when I needed it."

I hear her yelling as I walk out, get into the truck and slam the door, heading off to the nearest cheap motel where I can get a room for the rest of my leave.

This place is toxic, and I don't plan on coming back.

CHAPTER 7

ELAINE

This is one depressing motel room. Looking around at the orange and gold monstrosity around me, it just hurts my heart. After the blow up with his mom yesterday, my parents offered to let him stay in our guest room again, but he declined. Part of it is he wants privacy for us and I'm sure part of it is embarrassment. I know he acts like his parents being shitty is nothing to him, but I can tell it's bothering him.

My plan is to cheer him up, though. I went to the mall with a couple of the girls I've met at college and they helped me pick out a cute nighty. I hope he likes it, he went to get us some pizza and I jumped at the chance to slip it on. When I hear the key in the lock, I do my best to give him a sexy pose.

His eyes shoot up and he sits the pizza on the small table. "Well, this is a nice surprise."

I raise myself up to my knees and curl my finger, calling him over. He steps in front of me, kissing me hard and then running his finger along the strap of the nighty. "This is sexy, but it's in the way."

He reaches down, pulling it over my head. I yelp and I'm left in the very small panties it came with. His mouth finds my breast and his teeth tug lightly at my nipple. "Fuck, baby, you're so sexy."

"Oh god!" I call out as I start to grab for his shirt but he takes over, snatching it over his head while I push his pants and boxers down.

Grabbing me under the arms, he tosses me back on the bed. "Oh!" I call out before he starts crawling over me, kissing down my breast bone to the top of my panties. He grabs the small strings on the sides and snaps them, tossing the panties to the side. His fingers run over the patch of dark brown curls between my legs. I buck off the bed, but he presses me down before putting his mouth on me.

He begins to lick and suck on the small bundle of nerves between my thighs. "Damn, you taste so good, baby."

"Oh god, please don't stop." I feel my body start to tighten and tingle before I scream out to Vance, God and anyone in the near vicinity that may be listening.

"That's it, baby." He leans up, grabbing a condom from the nightstand and rolling it on. Reaching under my legs, he pulls me to him, slamming into me.

I cry out and the sound of our bodies slapping together takes over the room. This isn't making love, this is fucking. It's naughty, it's raw and it's dirty.

He drops my legs and leans over me, tensing up and kissing my neck before we both come.

As he lies on top of me, I let out a small laugh.

"What are you laughing about? Guys get nervous when you do that while they're practically still inside of you."

I shake my head. "Nothing, we were just very dirty."

He kisses my lips, "And I intend to be that dirty again after we eat."

Eating our now cold pizza and watching TV in our sweats is comfortable. I don't feel nervous or worried about how he's looking at me, because I know it's only me. I do worry about him, though, he's being a little distant. I mean not when we're having sex, but like his head is somewhere else. I'm sure he's thinking about training or something. Maybe I need to go with him when he leaves. Maybe that's what I'm supposed to do.

I reach over and touch his hand. "Hey."

He glances at me. "Yeah?"

"I was just wondering," I take a deep breath before I continue, "I've missed you so much while you've been gone. I was thinking maybe I could move up there and go to school, be near you." I run my hand over my face. "God, I sound so needy."

He chuckles. "No, you don't. I like the idea that you want to be near me, but maybe we should wait a little bit longer. I have to go to ITB and then I'm planning on trying to get into sniper school. That's gonna be months of training. I don't want you in a strange town while I can't be there. You've got school and you want your career."

While I know we weren't originally planning to continue with things, I don't know, I find myself disappointed. I feel the flush creeping up on my face. He doesn't want me there. This was always just supposed to be on the surface. Yes, we've said promising things to each other, but nothing about moving in together. I am so stupid, but I can't help it. It breaks my heart when he's gone, it breaks my heart that he doesn't want me there. "So, you want me to just stay here?" My voice betrays me with a quiver.

He reaches over and brushes the hair from my face. "Just for a little while longer. I will come back for you, but I don't know that I'll be settled for a little while longer. It may be a year before I'm somewhere for more than a few months at a time, and remember that'll only be for a few years since orders are two to three years per duty station. Hell, normally your first station is your hardship station. I could end up on a boat or some damn base I can't bring someone to." His face looks distant and unsure.

"I don't care, I'll follow you everywhere," I say before I can think.

"Just give me some time." He kisses my forehead. "Okay, babe?"

I nod and kiss him on the lips because honestly, I don't know what I'm supposed to think, say, or do. "Okay."

"So what's your schedule tomorrow?" he asks, pulling me closer.

"I have classes until lunch, and then a study group right after, it's normally like an hour, but then I'm free," I say, smiling.

"Where is your study group and I'll pick you up from there?" He's been using my car since he returned my dad's truck.

"We get together at a little café by the college. I'll write down the address in the morning."

"Do you want me to take you home or are you staying the night with me?" he says with a little smirk.

"I'm staying here. Dad has to cover part of next shift so he'll be working until five in the morning and my bedroom door is shut so he'll just think I'm sleeping. Mom said she'd cover for me."

"Are you sure? I don't want to piss off your dad. He's been good to me." His face shows his true worry.

"It's gonna be fine. Dad will go straight to bed when he comes in because he has to do the same thing tomorrow night. Mom knows we're missing each other, she's not super happy with it, but she says she understands," I explain.

He nods. "Okay. Let's get some shuteye."

I turn to him. "Hey."

"Yeah," he says to the ceiling.

"I love you," I whisper.

He rotates to me and pulls me tight. "I love you, too."

~*~

Normally, I enjoy my classes but today feels like it's taking forever. I even debate skipping my study session, but I know better. I'd fall so far behind and these courses are tough. If I work hard and finish as many as I can, maybe by the time he's somewhere I can go, I'll have my degree. Then, maybe I'll be able to go with him and be ready to work.

Finally walking into the café, I go to the corner where my study group always sits. I see a few of my normal group already there. "Hey, guys." I give a small wave as I sit down.

Everyone waves a hello. Lacey stands up to hug me and introduces me to a new face, I'm guessing. "Elaine, this is Jeff, he's taking a few classes with me for his degree. He's doing prerequisites for medical, so he got stuck in a couple of our classes. I told him our study group rocked so he asked if he could join."

I reach out to shake his hand. "Hi, I'm Elaine Loxley, nice to meet you."

He returns the handshake, "Jeffery Storm, nice to meet you, too."

We sit down and get started on our studies, after an hour I'm ready for Vance to come pick me up. He should be walking through the door any moment. I feel someone touch my shoulder and turn to see Jeffery. "So, I was wondering if you'd like to grab dinner sometime?"

"I'm sorry, I have a boyfriend."

Lacey laughs, "Yes and we get to meet this hot Marine boyfriend today, right?"

I laugh, "Yes, he should be here anytime now."

As if he heard me, he walks through the door. I can feel my face warm up from the smile. "Hey, babe," he says, pulling me into his arms.

"Hey," I say, giving him a quick kiss on the cheek. "I want you to meet some of my study group. A few have left, but this is my friend Lacey, Michele, Sarah, John and our new member, Jeffery. Everyone, this is my boyfriend Vance."

He gives everyone a wave and exchanges pleasantries. John speaks up, "Man, you have an awesome girl here. She's super smart, I don't think we'd know what to do without her."

Vance laughs, "Yeah, she's always been the smart one."

"Sure seems like it." This comes from Jeffery and he's smiling at me. Surely he's not going to make eyes at me in front of Vance. I mean you'd have to be stupid. Vance was always great looking but holy shit, since he went into the Marines he's built. I also never thought I'd like him with short hair, but the haircut only adds to the badass look that's him now.

I grab Vance's hand. "Come on, let's go."

"It was nice meeting all of you," he says to the group.

Lacey tugs me so she can speak in my ear. "Holy shit, girl, you go take care of your business with him while he's here."

I laugh as I pull away and we walk out of the café. "Where to?" he says.

"I don't care as long as we're together," I say with a smile.

~*~

I hear a pounding and I feel Vance move beside me. I rub my eyes and sit up just as he's pulling on his boxers to answer the door. I reach beside the bed and slide on his t-shirt just before he opens the door.

I see my father standing on the other side and wish this bed would swallow me. He makes eye contact with me but only for a second. "Vance, we need to talk for a minute, get dressed." My dad steps away from the door to give us a little privacy, I'm guessing.

Vance pulls on a pair of jeans and another t-shirt, while I grab my shorts I had on earlier. I quickly grab the couple of condom wrappers on the nightstand and throw them in the trash. He looks at me as if he's asking if I'm ready before calling my father in. Am I ready? Hell no, my father is about to come through that door and he knows what I've been doing. There is no way to hide this. I'm worried he's going to lose it when he gets in here.

My dad takes a seat in the cheap motel chair. "I wish I were here for different reasons," he says in his gruff, no-nonsense cop voice. It's always wowed me how my father's voice can go from the warm man I know at home to the dry, void voice when he's in cop mode.

Vance sits on the edge of the bed. "Okay." I take a seat beside him.

"I gotta call just a little while ago. Apparently, your parents were having an argument."

Vance shakes his head. "Go figure. So, you had to lock one or both of them up." There is this pause and I swear somehow the air in the room grows thick. I can't explain it, but something shifts.

"No, son. We haven't figured out the exact details yet, but there was a gun. From what investigators are gathering, at some point, your mother was shot and your dad turned it on himself." I hear my breath catch. "We don't know if he had the gun all along or if he was taking it from her. Right now, unfortunately, we just know the end results."

Vance's face pales and he looks at the ceiling and takes in a deep breath. "I knew something like this would happen sooner or later." Once he looks back at my dad I can see the glassiness in his eyes. I know they were shitty people, but they were still his parents. I feel the tension radiating off of him.

My dad shakes his head. "Like I said, son, I wish I were here for different reasons, but I wanted to be the one to come and tell you myself."

"What, um…what do I need to do?"

My dad takes a breath. "Well, right now they've been moved to the coroner's office for an autopsy and the investigation. We generally know what happened, but with cases like this, we have a protocol to follow. I have explained to them that we need to expedite this as much as possible because of your training."

Vance nods. "I appreciate that." He shakes his head. "I'm sure they didn't have any money or life insurance."

"We'll get you some information on what you can do in the morning. Try to get some sleep and then both of you have yourselves at my house for breakfast." There it is, the dad tone. He's not going to let it slip that I'm here.

After he leaves we try to settle back in, but sleep really doesn't come for either of us. Right before daylight, he brushes his lips to mine. "I need you right now."

"Okay."

"I need you hard. I need to not think of anything but you for just a little while."

I nod as he pushes the shirt up I'm wearing and sucks my nipple into his mouth roughly. I cry out as he pushes my panties down my legs. Reaching between us, he rubs my clit hard and fast, bringing me to the brink and then pulling away. Before I can complain, he's lined his cock up with my entrance and thrusts inside me. "Oh god, Vance!"

He slides my legs up to his shoulders and grabs around my thighs, slamming into me hard and fast. The only thing I can hear over the sounds of our bodies slapping is my screams of pleasure. "Holy shit! I'm gonna, I'm gonna, oh my god!" Before I can come down, he snatches out of me and hot ropes of cum fly all over my stomach.

He falls on the bed beside me. "Sorry, I forgot to get a condom."

I give a little laugh, "Okay. I was just wondering if it was something new you're into."

His laugh is short and gruff. "No, but I can tell you, that feeling of my cock inside you without anything separating us is as close to heaven as I'll ever get." He kisses me on the lips, but it's quick. "We need to get you cleaned up and get to your house. I'm sure your dad is gonna rip my balls off."

I laugh as we get up. "I hope not, I'm kinda partial to them." Hopefully for just a few more minutes we can forget everything looming over us. His parents' deaths and my dad's wrath.

As we drive over to my parents', he seems like he's off on another planet. I'm sure if I were in his shoes I'd be the same way, though. I let out a deep sigh when we pull into my parents' driveway at seven sharp. "Let's do this," I say before we get out. Going through the front door, I'm met with the look from my mom that says I've absolutely lost my mind, but in the same moment she turns to Vance with nothing but sympathy.

She pulls him into a hug. "Vance, honey, I'm so sorry."

"Thanks, but it's okay, they weren't really…you know," he replies, shrugging it off.

We walk into my parents' kitchen where breakfast is on the table. My mom must've just put everyone's eggs on their plates since they were still steaming. Dad's plate has two fried eggs along with Vance's plate being the same. Hers and mine have one each. A pot of grits and a plate of bacon and biscuits sits in the middle. I take my usual seat, dishing some grits on top of my eggs before grabbing a biscuit and a few pieces of bacon.

My dad sits down as I mix my grits and eggs. "First, let's go over the obvious. I am not happy that I found you staying with Vance in the motel, but you're eighteen years old and I can't make your decisions for you. I know that you and Vance mean a lot to each other, but I don't like being slapped in the face with it. So, with that said, as long as you live here, no more sleepovers." The tone is no-nonsense which means it's not up for discussion, not that I have a rebuttal at the ready anyway. "Now," he continues, "we have more important things to discuss…" That leads into him telling Vance what all he'll have to do about his parents.

"Can I just have them cremated?" I hear my mom gasp.

My dad shrugs and looks at him thoughtfully, "Yeah, you can."

Vance looks around the table and expels a breath that it seems he's been holding in. "For most of my life they told me I was worthless and that if it wasn't for the extra food stamps they got for me, they'd have left me in an alley or something. Then they basically kill each other and leave me nothing to pay for it. I have a little money saved, but not a lot. So we can just cremate them and I'll figure out what to do with their ashes later."

My dad nods in understanding, my mom wipes silent tears from her face and my heart feels like it might explode in my chest. He sits here looking so distant and cold, but I can feel that little boy, the one who only wanted his parents to love him. The little boy who I watched at class parties when everyone else's parents came, but not his, or worse if they did, they were an embarrassment. All of that is flashing like a movie reel in my mind. At least thirteen years of memories and I realize, where it would tear me apart if something happened to one of my parents, I can totally understand where he just wants this to be over with.

After breakfast, Dad and Vance go out into the yard to talk about his parents' stuff and I sit in the living room with my mom.

She sits in her rocking chair reading a magazine. "You put me in a bad situation last night, Elaine." Her voice is tight, but not angry.

I sigh. "I'm sorry, I know." I stare at the wall by the door. "I want to go with him." I blurt out what I feel.

She shakes her head. "Baby, that's a hard life."

"I know, and he told me I have to wait anyway. He's not going to be in a place to have me there for at least a year," I explain, but I want her to understand I still plan to go.

"Are you sure you want a relationship like this?" she asks me, sighing.

"Just because you didn't want to go with Dad and let him travel the world and be able to experience part of it with him doesn't mean I don't want to." It comes out shorter than I intend for it to, but deep down I mean it.

She looks almost hurt. "Elaine, I never wanted to go with your dad because I wanted to build my life here. The other side of that is he also didn't want me traipsing all over the world after him. Yes, me staying here ended with him getting out and coming home, but that was his decision, I'd told him we could go our separate ways." With that she gets up and leaves the room.

I shake my head because my mom pretty much gave him an ultimatum if he wanted her, it really wasn't his decision like she says.

How can you make someone else's decision for them?

CHAPTER 8

MARCO

Sitting on the back patio with her dad, I feel like a piece of shit. "I'm sorry about last night, about you finding her with me at the motel."

He shakes his head. "You've got bigger things going on right now."

I shake my head, "No, I don't. She is one of the most important things in my life right now. Which is why this sucks. You know I respect the hell out of you, Mr. Loxley, which is why I need your help with this."

He looks at me like if he had his gun right now, he'd shoot me. "You aren't marrying my only child and snatching her around the world with you."

"I know that. I'm leaving in the morning to go back. I'm gonna get a bus ticket this afternoon. I can't stay here; this place is toxic for me. I'll leave you some money to take care of the funeral home. As far as my parents' stuff, if it's okay I'll stop by there this afternoon and grab a few things I might want to keep. Other than that, the rest can be thrown out or donated. I need you to help me get all of that done," I say, resting my face in my hands, my elbows braced on my knees.

He adjusts his neck. "What about Elaine?"

"She deserves more than some piece of shit from the trailer park who is going to spend the rest of his life moving from place to place like a gypsy."

"You're making something of yourself, son," he butts in. "You are not a piece of shit. I'm not in the habit of wasting my time on pieces of shit so don't talk about yourself that way. It makes me look like an idiot."

I shake my head. "No, you were right, I don't want her following me around the world when she can do so much better. I saw her yesterday with her friends in her study group. She doesn't know I watched her from outside for a while. Her face was so happy. She seemed so carefree. That's what I want for her. There were a couple of guys in the group with her. I could see her getting the life she wants. The job, the husband, the house, the kids, all of it right here, and the truth is, it's just not with me. It kills me but I want that for her."

He clears his throat. "What are you going to tell her?"

"I'm going to talk to her tonight, after I get my ticket. I hate this town. I hate my life here. I feel like I can't breathe. I do love her, but I love her enough I feel like I need to let her go," I try to explain. "Can you please just help me handle the other stuff?"

He stands up. "I'll take care of all of that for you. What do you want me to do with their ashes?"

"I honestly don't care. You can dump them in the toilet at the bar and I can promise you I won't lose any sleep over it."

He puts his hand out for me to shake and I do. "Listen, I have to go in to work in a little while so I'm going to take a nap. I know this is going to break her heart, but I also understand what you're trying to do, and I can admire that a little."

His hand still grasping mine, my voice shakes when I speak. "I just want what's best for her and that isn't me. I do want to say thank you for everything you've done for me. I'm not sure how much you'll hear from me after today. She probably won't want to talk to me and I'm not sure I'm strong enough to stay away from her if I keep in touch." I have a lump in my throat the size of a cantaloupe. My insides feel like they are going to explode. I wasn't even this upset when I found out about my parents. I'm a Marine, damnit, it shouldn't be this hard.

He nods but reaches in his pocket, pulling out his wallet and taking some card out of it. "Do me a favor, just for me, one jarhead to another." He hands me the card. "That's my address at the department, my number and my extension, make sure you keep in touch every once in a while. Okay? Like I said, I'm not in the habit of worrying about people who aren't worth my time, so if I say you are...you are."

I nod. "Yes, sir."

I sit outside, staring across her back yard until I hear the door open. I look up and she's walking my way smiling and it kills me that I know I'm going to break her heart. "Hey, I was wondering if he'd killed you back here."

"No, just enjoying the weather. I'm gonna head back to the motel and get a shower. I've got to call the funeral home and all. How about we go out to dinner tonight?"

She tilts her head. "Are you sure you don't want me to come with you?"

I can't let on that anything is worrying me. I just want one last good night with her. "No, you need to study and this is stuff I kinda need to do alone. I'll pick you up at six?"

She smiles, putting her arms around my neck. "Yeah, if you're sure."

I kiss the top of her head. "I am."

I make sure to pass back through the house and speak to her mom, giving her a hug and a thank you. I'm not sure when or if I'll see her after today and I want her to know what everything she's done means to me.

As I drive back to the motel, I wish my parents could've been more like the Loxleys. Getting out of my car and stepping into the old motel room, my heart aches a little. I can smell her. The last twenty-four hours have been a lot. My parents always knew how to ruin a great day. Although, seeing her in that café yesterday, that one guy obviously making eyes at her—at first it pissed me off, but then it hit me. I'm not what she needs, especially after our wakeup call last night. No matter what Hugh says, I am the trash everyone thought I was growing up, just like my parents, and she deserves the American dream. All of it.

I start gathering the few items I have with me, putting them in my sea bag. Feeling under the edge of the bed, I pull out a pair of tiny panties. I sit for a minute just holding them. And like a sick weirdo with a glutton for punishment, I slip them into the side of my bag. I'll keep this little piece of her. I go to the funeral home and set up everything for once my parents' bodies are released, giving them a check for part of it, until everything with the investigation is completed and leaving Hugh's contact information to settle the rest of it and anything else they need. I swing by the bus station on my way back to the motel and find out that they have a bus leaving at ten o'clock tonight. I go ahead and get my ticket. I was going to leave tomorrow, but after I break the news to Elaine I won't have a reason to stay any longer. I'm also not sure I'd still be strong enough to leave in the morning.

~*~

Sitting in one of the nicest restaurants in our town, I feel like a phony. We've just finished a great meal and now I have to break the heart of the only girl I've ever loved. "Are you okay?" she asks me from across the table. "I know everything with your parents has been a lot to deal with."

"I'm fine, just a lot going on up here," I say, pointing to my head.

Once the waiter brings back my change, I stand up and we make our way through the restaurant to the car. Once we're inside, I reach over the console and kiss her hard.

"Lainey, I need to talk to you," I say, still holding her face.

She looks scared. "O-okay."

My mind races. Can I really break her heart like I'm about to? This is what's better for her, though. That's what I have to keep telling myself. Rip off the band-aid. "I'm leaving on a bus in two hours."

Shock is what I see in her eyes. "What? I thought you had a few more days. We were going to take you back." Her voice is quivering.

Watching her, knowing I'm killing us both inside, it breaks me, but I press on.

"Lainey, I can't stay here. This place is bad for me." I look around at nothing so I don't cry and look like a total pussy. "I think it's best if we break this off now."

Her body shakes. "What?! No!"

I reach over and touch her face. "I have to do this. You deserve better."

Tears start rolling down her face. "I'll wait for you."

"I don't want you to." For the second or third time today, a first in more years than I can count, I feel emotions clogging my throat. "You need to move on with your life here. I don't want you tied down to me. You deserve to be happy, with a career, a husband, kids, all of it. You can't get that from me. I wasn't lying to you earlier when I told you that I'd be in training for a while. I'm hoping to get selected for sniper school. If that happens I'll be gone more than I'm home. To be honest, I never see myself coming back here and I know your family is important to you, and for good reason. I could never ask you to be away from them that much."

I swipe at the tears that are rolling down her face and her face shifts to a little bit of anger. "I love you, Vance. You can't make this decision for me. Was that what the sex this morning was about? A goodbye fuck?" Her voice is raised now.

I pull her into my chest. "Yes and no. I'll always want you, but I can't have you anymore. Don't you see my life here is a train wreck? I know you'd go with me and maybe we'd be happy for a while, but it's not what you deserve."

She pulls away from me. "Fine," she replies, looking out the window. "You've made up your mind and I don't get a say in it."

I'm dying here. "I know this is a lot to ask, but please don't hate me. I love you, too, which is why I'm doing this."

She looks at me and whispers, "I could never hate you. I just wish you had more faith in me, in us."

I crank the car, unable to reply. "Let's go sit for a little while and then you can drop me off."

She looks at her lap. "Okay."

I decide to just go ahead and drive to the bus station. We can sit in the parking lot there. We don't speak on the way or when we park. I drum my nervous fingers on the steering wheel. "I want you to know I've never loved another girl."

She snorts, "If you love me so much how can you walk away from me? Don't you see this is killing me? I'm dying inside right now, Vance! Please, don't do this to me, to us." Her voice is shredded.

For the first time since I was maybe five or six, tears roll down my face. "I do love you that much! Can't you see that? You deserve better."

"Shut the fuck up!" she screams. "I'm tired of you telling me what you think I deserve. What about you? You deserve to be happy, too. I know you don't think that and it's really messed up, but you do." I shake my head and she opens the car door. "Don't shake your head at me, and stop making decisions for me."

She walks around the car and snatches my door open. "Get out."

I get out and pull her into me, feeling her resistance. "I do love you, more than anything."

"Well, then stay here for the next few days like we planned. We'll find a way to work this out, together." I know one day I'll probably regret the hell out of what I'm doing, but it can't be today. I turn our bodies so her back is ready to go in the car. I pull back and shake my head. "I can't." I reach in the back seat and grab my duffle. "You'll thank me for this when you get the life you've always wanted."

I turn and walk away. From inside the station, I watch as she crumples into the car sobbing, before she finally pulls away.

CHAPTER 9

ELAINE

Spring 1990

God, I hate having to ask my dad for money, but after throwing up just before getting off my shift this morning I don't have a choice, my insurance won't kick in for another couple of months. The doctor on shift told me I had to go see my doctor and make sure I'm not contagious. It takes every bit of strength I have after a twelve-hour shift at the hospital to walk into his office at the department. I knock on the door frame. "Hey, Daddy."

"Hey, my favorite daughter," he says, standing up to hug me.

"I'm your only daughter," I say before I glance down at his desk. Laying on his desk, I see a letter with familiar handwriting. Handwriting I haven't seen in a long time, but I'd know it anywhere.

I had a feeling my dad was keeping in touch with him. At first, I thought it was just stuff to do with his parents' deaths, but now I think it's more. I point to the letter. "So you've been keeping in touch with Vance?"

He shrugs, folding up the letter. "In a way. He drops me a line or two every so often, like when he's leaving or coming in from a mission."

I take a seat in front of his desk. It hurts that he left and hasn't sent me anything, but he still talks to my dad. It pisses me off because I thought I'd moved on after him.

"So is he coming or going?"

"Just got in, but probably gearing up to leave again soon. Being a sniper keeps you busy," he explains, but doesn't really give me any details and my heart still can't take asking for any.

I started dating Jeffery a few months after Vance left, I was trying to do what Vance told me and I was so lonely. He said all of the right things and did all of the right things.

Then we got married, and at first it was great, I was still finishing up my classes and he'd dropped out to take a job to support us until I graduated. Little by little the pieces started falling apart. I got grants and took out student loans for classes and books. Every job he got he didn't keep for long, just enough to keep the rent paid, usually a month late, and the power on, but that was always right before they cut if off. I can't tell you how many meals I've had at my parents' house just so we could eat. How many times I internally did somersaults when my mom would insist I take home leftovers. As soon as I got my job at the hospital a few months ago, he didn't even bother looking for another job. So, he just sits at home all day now. I keep encouraging him to go back and finish his degree and he refuses. He says it's my fault he never finished and now he feels too old to go back. Too old my ass, he's twenty-one years old, not forty. Days like today I wonder what in the hell Vance was thinking when he thought I'd be better off here.

"So what brings you by today?" he says, taking his seat.

I sigh. "I got sick at work today, I was almost at the end of my shift and I just started throwing up. So they sent me home and told me to go see my regular doctor to make sure I'm not contagious. My problem is my insurance doesn't kick in for a little longer and I just don't have the fifty dollars to go to the doctor. Is there any way you can loan it to me?"

He nods and I can tell he's dying to say something not nice. "Okay. I'll give you the fifty dollars. Has Jeff had any job leads?"

I sigh. "No, I don't think so. At this point I'm honestly not sure he's even looking. Daddy, I'm trying so hard to make this work." I've covered for Jeff with my parents for a while now, but I just don't have it in me to do it anymore.

His face softens a little, I'm sure he's been seeing how unhappy I am and just didn't say anything.

"Sweetheart, I know you are, but sometimes you just can't save things. Sometimes they're not worth saving either."

"Daddy, we haven't even been married two years yet." It's hard for me to admit defeat. I mean if I can't fix this with Jeff, I'll feel like a two-time loser. I couldn't keep Vance either.

"I just don't want you to get ten years down the road from now with a house full of kids that you're raising yourself, because his ass won't go to work. I haven't said anything because your mom told me not to. But I can't look at you sitting across from me and see how tired you are, how sad you look and how run down you are, and keep my mouth shut anymore."

I wipe some tears that were forming in the corner of my eyes. "I know, Daddy, but I need to salvage this. I've already lost Vance, I can't lose Jeff, too."

He gets up from his chair and walks around the desk to pull me up in his arms. "Sweetie, Vance did what he had to do. Honestly, it really didn't have anything to do with you. It was all him and what he had going on in his head. Here's the thing, though, you can't keep supporting some jackass who won't get off the damn couch."

"Well, he did support me while I was in school."

He pulls back, looking me in the face. "Yes, while you were in school and you worked part-time. You weren't sitting at the house just making hot air."

I pull away and take a step back. "I know, Daddy. I've got a lot to think about. Right now, I just want to go home and sleep until I see the doctor later this afternoon."

"They got you in today?"

I nod, "Yeah, I need to work tonight, so I gotta get that note."

"Can you swap shifts with someone? Get some rest?"

"I'll be fine. I just need to get home and sleep."

He reaches in his desk drawer and gets out his checkbook. He scribbles in it before tearing out a check. "Here, sweetie. I made it out to you."

I look at the check for one hundred dollars. "Daddy, I only need fifty dollars."

"Yeah, but you may need medicine. So, I did a little extra."

I hug him hard. "Thank you, Daddy."

"You're welcome, and you think about what we talked about. If you need your mom or me, you let us know."

I sigh and lean back against his desk. "I just don't want to be a disappointment to you guys. You guys never fight, you were never separated and you're always there for each other."

He tips my face up to look at him. "You could never be a disappointment to us. You've given it your best. It's not always been perfect between your mom and me, we've had tough times, but we were both willing participants in our marriage. We both worked for it."

I give him another hug and then head home to rest. Once I get home, I find that Jeff is still in bed and my house is messy. Beer cans on my coffee table and counter. I start grabbing them up and I notice what looks like lipstick or something on the rim. I'm too tired to worry right now. Tossing all of them in the trash, I head to the bedroom and crawl into bed beside my husband.

A few hours later, I'm up getting ready to go to the doctor. "Why are you leaving so early?" Jeff asks.

"I have to go to the doctor, I got sick at work last night and they won't let me go back in without a note from my doctor saying I'm not contagious. Then I'm going to work."

He nods. "How much is that going to cost me?"

That irritates me, he wants to know how much it's going to cost him! "Not a damn thing."

"What does that mean?"

My frustration is at an all-time high. First of all, my dad gave me the money and second, he'd have to be contributing for it to cost him.

"Nothing, I'll see you later." I snatch my purse off the counter and go out to my car.

~*~

Sitting in the treatment room, I wait for Dr. Broome to come in. When he steps in, I'm relieved. "Okay, Dr. Broome, can I just get a note that says I'm not going to get anyone sick so I can get to work?"

He nods. "Yeah, what you have isn't contagious."

I stand up and grab my bag. "Okay, great. I'll see you later."

"Wait, Elaine, I need to give you a prescription."

"For what? If I'm not contagious I don't need anything." I can't afford to be paying for meds for nothing.

"You're not, but you do need some prenatal vitamins," he says, leveling his eyes at me.

I back up until my legs hit the chair and I sit down. "Wh-what?"

"I take it you weren't expecting that news?" he asks.

I shake my head. "No. Not at all. I've been on birth control."

"Well, that's not always effective and many things can interfere with it."

I shake my head. "I know, I know. I'm a nurse, how did I not see this?"

"Well, you're probably not that far along, you told the nurse that your cycle even with the pill is not always regular."

I nod. "Yeah, the new pill they put me on at my last visit has made it so sometimes I completely skip my period." I think back to the last time I had a period. "I think my last period was two months ago."

He nods, "Okay, well, you should set up an appointment with your OBGYN and get an ultrasound, see how far along you are."

I take a deep breath and stand up. How am I going to pay for this? "Thank you for letting me know. I'll make that appointment." After I double-check the date my insurance kicks in and maybe make it right after that date, so it'll be covered.

After I leave his office, I go straight to work. Walking around the hospital, I feel like I'm in a fog. Dr. Franz, one of the surgeons who is new, stops me in the hall. "Elaine, you still don't look good."

"I'm fine, though."

"I know Greg sent you home this morning."

"I brought in a note from my doctor. I'm fine."

He pulls me into a room. "You're far from fine. You look like you're about to drop. You need to go home and rest."

I shake my head. "I'm not contagious, I'm fine. I need to work." I'm going to have a baby. I need to take care of it.

"Elaine, you will be no good to us if you pass out on the floor, whether you're contagious or not."

I'm so tired of people being in my damn business. "I'm not sick, I'm pregnant." Shit. I didn't want to tell anyone.

"Well, congratulations!"

My eyes water, "I just found out, I haven't told anyone." He pulls me into his chest. "Hey, don't cry. I take it that this isn't what you were planning."

I shake my head and sob. "No, I'm hoping I can hold off on my first OB appointment until my insurance kicks in."

He pats my back like a small child, "It will all work out. I'm sure we can find out about the insurance, you just take good care of yourself, start taking some prenatal vitamins, stay hydrated and you should be able to wait a few weeks before going in." He waves one of his hands around. "You just so happen to work at a really great hospital, if we think something is wrong, I'll take a look or ask one of my friends to. We do have ultrasound machines here. I'm sure we can figure something out. The biggest thing is I don't want you stressing about it. Why don't you go on home? It's a slow night. Take the time, talk about it with your husband."

"I don't want to talk to him," I say, wiping my face.

He rubs my arm. "Elaine, go home, talk to him."

I sigh, I know he's right. "Okay."

"You'll feel better after you talk to him about it." I doubt it, but I don't say it.

I clock out and make my way home. It's ten at night and all of the lights are on. "Well, he slept all day, he should be awake now," I say to myself as I get out of my car.

Opening the front door, I find him on the couch, the beer cans are all around and a woman is in his lap. I slam the door. "Pardon me, can you get the fuck off my husband?"

She jumps up and grabs her clothes. "You said she wouldn't be home tonight!"

Anger, anger, anger, that's what fills me. I want to snatch her up by her fucking hair, but it's not just me anymore. "Oh darn," I say. "Shit happens. Now, you skanky homewrecker, get the fuck out of my house." I step toward her and she flinches.

Before I can say anything else, she runs out without her shoes. I reach down and grab them, throwing them out the door behind her. Jeffery looks at me and he's mad.

"What in the hell are you doing home early?" His voice sounds annoyed.

My anger is boiling over. No denial, no sorry, it was the first time, no remorse. "Well, I don't have to answer to you. I know you're worried I'll be short a few hours on my check and you won't be able to buy your normal beer so that you can sit at home and stink up the fucking couch, but too bad. Life is about to change around here. I'm going to my parents' for the night, when I come back in the morning you better be up and sober. I just found out that I'm pregnant, so our life isn't just about us anymore."

He jumps up, his dick flopping in the wind. "What do you mean pregnant?"

"I mean that one of the last few times we had sex resulted in me getting pregnant, even on my pills. But thanks to you I guess when I go to the OBGYN I can get tested for STDs as well."

"Fuck you, Elaine. Your ass ain't never here to take care of me. Look at this damn house, and as far as sex goes, you lack a lot." He's snatching on his pants. "You're getting rid of it, right? I don't need a damn kid right now."

Rage, that's what I feel, fucking rage. I pick up a vase off the shelf and throw it at him, just missing his fat head. It shatters on the wall behind him. "Let me tell you something, you fucking piece of shit. This is my baby and I will not be getting rid of it. If I get rid of anyone, it's you. This house is a fucking wreck because you are a worthless pig and sorry if working twelve hours a day to support your sorry ass makes me too tired to fuck your limp dick. Like I said, I'm going to my parents' tonight. We'll talk more tomorrow."

I walk out to my car and slam the door after getting in. Taking a deep breath, I drive to my parents'. I have some decisions to make tonight and it's not going to be easy. As I pull away, I rub my hand on the dash where the scratches are still from mine and Vance's initials before he left for boot camp. It hits me, I'm not even that mad that he was fucking around. It's not like we've had a great sex life, it's the betrayal. The fact that he brought another woman into my house. The fact that he doesn't appreciate anything I do. The fact that he's just an overall piece of shit.

Then again, the decisions could be easier than I think.

CHAPTER 10

MARCO

February 1991- End of Desert Storm

All of that bullshit for forty-three days. I will say, though, what my teacher said when I was little is the truth. When I was in elementary school and learning to spell desert and dessert, that the key was the s's. She said, "Always remember you want two helpings of dessert and to only go to the desert once." That statement is the damn truth.

The bad part is we did very little to neutralize what we needed to, we just put out a small fire. We left a man in charge who is going to make major problems for the world. Mark my words, we'll be back there sooner or later for the same fight.

I sit here going through all of my mail that piled up while I was gone and come across a letter from my hometown. Hugh Loxley has done his best to keep his tabs on me. He's a good man and I respect the hell out of him, that's the reason I keep in touch with him and no one else from there. If I had more willpower, I'd keep in touch with Elaine, but I just can't. I know she's married, and that Hugh hates her husband, thinks he's a sorry piece of shit. I knew the day I met that dipshit in the café he was sketchy. I had hopes, though. With a good woman like Elaine, how could he not treat her right?

Opening the envelope, I pull out the letter and a picture falls out. It's Elaine asleep on the couch with a baby on her chest. Written across the bottom it says Loxley Michael Storm. I can't bring myself to read his letter today. The sight of her with a baby tears me apart more than I could ever prepare myself for. She's beautiful even sleeping, I always knew she was meant to be a mother and a caretaker. My heart always wonders if it was the dumbest decision I ever made to let her go, that could be my son on her chest, but in my head I know she deserves the life she's getting. She deserves that beautiful baby on her chest and a husband that isn't moving them from place to place. My chest feels like it's about to split open and I want to break things, before I do I put it all back in the envelope and call my friend Beck.

"Hello."

"Hey, Beck, it's DeMarco."

"What's going on, man?"

"I need to drink tonight. You coming with me?"

"Sure, you wanna go to the NCO Club or off base?"

"Off base, I have a feeling I'm going to be an idiot and I don't want to do it here."

"Okay, man, I'll be at your place in twenty. I'll be the DD so you can tell me what's going on."

"Roger."

~*~

Sitting at the bar, I tell him about the letter. "Man, you have pined over this girl for too long. She has a husband and a kid. You gotta move on. At your three o'clock there is a woman who hasn't taken her eyes off of you since we walked in."

I glance over and see a beautiful Latino woman and she is looking at me hard. He shoves my shoulder. "You should go talk to her, and don't do like you've done with other women. Fuck them and compare them to Elaine. You've got to move on for real."

He's right. I stand up and make my way over to the beauty looking my way. "Hey, can I buy you a drink?" How original, I know.

She grins. "Sure, that'd be great."

I flag the bartender down and tell him what we want. "So, beautiful, what's your name?"

She smiles. "Rosalinda, and yours?"

"Vance DeMarco."

She rubs her hand across mine. "Nice to meet you, Vance."

"You, too."

Our conversation starts out small, but it's enough to keep us talking for a while.

Several drinks later, we're slow dancing as she licks my neck, and my cock is straining in my pants. "Let's get some air," I tell her.

Grabbing her hand, she follows me outside. I pull us around the edge of the building and pick her up under her ass. "You're so fucking sexy." I put her back against the wall to give us some support.

She moans. "You make me so hot."

Taking a hand loose, I slip under the skirt she's wearing and find her wet center. "Fuck, you're soaked."

"Fuck me right here, Vance. Fuck me so hard."

Steadying her legs back on the ground, I reach back under her skirt and rip her panties off, all while she unbuttons my jeans and shoves them down my hips. Lifting her back up, I slam into her wet core. "Oh, that's it, Vance, fuck me so hard."

It's a raw, rough, furious fuck. She screams as she comes and I realize I'm not wearing a rubber. I snatch out just in time to paint the wall behind her with my cum. Once I let her down, we both try to catch our breath. "You're beautiful."

"Thank you."

"What's your number? I wanna do this again and I really liked talking to you."

She looks scared for a moment. "You can't call me."

"Why not?"

"I'm sort of married."

I step back and tuck my dick in my pants. "Married?! How are you sort of married? What the fuck?"

"Listen, I want to leave him. But it's not that simple."

"What do you mean not that simple?"

"Well, he's kind of important in certain circles and he can make my life hell."

"Where is he so important?"

"Well, he's a colonel on base," she explains.

Time stands still.

My eyes bug out. "A colonel on this base? What's his name?"

"James Haas."

I rub my hands over my face. "My fucking colonel? You're fucking kidding me right now, aren't you?"

"Look, Vance, I really like you. I plan to leave him. I just have to get some things sorted."

"You realize this could cost me my fucking career, right?"

She steps closer to me, "It doesn't have to. We can keep this quiet until I can leave him. It was so easy to talk to you tonight. He treats me like a possession, not a person. He fucks around on me all the time. That's what originally brought me here tonight. I caught him again. I wasn't expecting to meet anyone, but there you were and I actually felt like a person again. Someone who was worth a conversation, someone worth flirting with. I'm just a fixture in his world, no more important than a painting on the wall."

She's crying now and I feel bad for her, but this is so fucked up. We had a connection tonight when we were talking. I can't help it, anytime a woman cries over something I've done I think about Elaine and how I never want to make someone cry like that again. I reach out to her and pull her to my chest, brushing her hair with my hand. "What are you going to do? I can't be a part of this until you're finished with him."

"Just give me some time and I'll be ready."

I nod. "Okay." I take her hand. "Let me walk you to your car, get me a piece of paper and a pen, I'll give you my number. You call me if you need me."

She smiles. "Okay."

~*~

I didn't plan on being with her again until she was actually separated, but then he left on a trip and she came over. Before I knew it, this has become a regular occurrence. I think it's more than sex for us, though, I really care about her. Beck tells me every chance he gets that I'm a fucking idiot and that my dick is going to get me killed. Hell, he's leaving me, though, his enlistment is up and he's already applied and been accepted to University of Florida.

Reaching over in my bed, I rub my hand up and down her arm while she sleeps. Her sigh is intoxicating. I dream of waking up to her for the rest of my life. I never thought I'd get over Elaine, but Rosalinda has given me hope.

"Hmm." Her eyes pop open, "Oh shit, Vance, you let me fall asleep again." She jumps from the bed and quickly dresses. "Do you want us to get caught?"

I sit up with my sheet around my waist. "Well, if you would file those papers we wouldn't have to worry about it."

"You know I can't do that right now. We have the Marine Corps Birthday Ball coming up. I just need more time. But soon, I promise." She leans over and kisses me hard before she walks out the door. It's been almost a year now, I'm not sure how much more time I can give her.

I stand up and watch out the window as she gets in her car to leave. After she pulls away, I notice a car leave a minute or so behind her. It could be a coincidence, but I don't believe in them.

~*~

I haven't heard from her in two weeks, but she's here and looking beautiful tonight. I hope at some point I can sneak in some talking to her. I know she's been busy with helping to plan this, but I can't help but wonder if we've been caught.

After dinner is over, I make my way to the bar and almost walk into her husband. "Excuse me, Colonel."

"No problem, Sergeant, I believe you know my wife, Rosalinda." He pulls her to his side with a smirk on his face. So yes, we've been caught.

Before I can say anything, he pulls her away. I need to get out of this building. I go take a walk in the gardens outside. Sitting on a bench and watching the stars, for the first time in a long time I think about Elaine. I wonder if her husband has stepped up any. I never did go back and read Hugh's last letter. I needed to close that chapter of my life for good.

"Vance," I hear whispered to me.

I turn to see her hiding behind a trellis. "Rosa, what the fuck?" I whisper back before stepping back there and pulling her into my arms.

"He was having me followed. After the last time I was at your place he lost it. He told me if I left him he'd make sure I ended up on the damn streets without a penny to my name and if I even thought about moving in with you he'd make sure you were dishonorably discharged and lose everything. We can't do this anymore."

I brush her face with my hands. "I won't let you take this from him."

She shakes her head. "You have to." I kiss her hard and we lose control. I pull her into an alcove where no one can see us. She fumbles with my dress belt and pants to push them down as I lift her up, shoving my cock inside her. "Oh god, Vance. I love you. I can't keep you, but I love you."

"Fuck, you're mine. Fuck him," I say as I thrust into her hard and fast. "I love you, too," I say with my final thrust, spilling inside of her.

We fix ourselves to walk back toward the ball that I have no intention of reentering. "I'm going to visit my mother tomorrow," she tells me. "I'll be back in two weeks."

"Okay, I'll see you then."

Or that was my intention anyway.

CHAPTER 11

ELAINE

September 1996

"How was your day at school, big man?" I ask my five-year-old son in the back seat of my car.

"It was good. My friend's Sly and Huck got in trouble for saying bad words in front of Mrs. Anders."

I try not to laugh, "Oh, they did. What did they say?"

He shakes his head, his brown hair flopping around. "I'm not gonna say."

"You can tell me, you won't get into trouble."

"Uh uh. No way."

I laugh, "Okay, well we have to stop at the grocery store on our way home. Gran needs some stuff for supper before I go to work."

"I wish you didn't always have to work at night."

"I know, me too, but hopefully soon I'll get the day shift."

Pulling into the parking lot of the Save-n-More, I find a spot and get out, meeting Lox as he opens his door. "Okay, you know the rules, hold my hand and no running off."

He nods. "Yes, ma'am."

Walking in the store, he points to two little boys beating up a quarter machine. "Those are my friends, Sly and Huck." He calls out to them. "Hey, Sly, hey, Huck."

The two little boys come running over to us and I look around for a mom to be following them. "Hey, Lox," one of them says. "We were trying to see if someone left a quarter in the machine. No luck." They're cute for sure.

I squat down. "Hi, guys, I'm Lox's mommy, who are you here with?"

The same twin speaks up. "Our mom, but she told us to leave her alone and let her shop."

"Oh, okay." Holy crap, this woman must be a real winner.

"So which one of you little guys is Sly and which one is Huck?" I ask, trying to make conversation until hopefully their mom gets here.

"I'm Sly," the same one speaks, "and this is Huck. He don't talk a lot and we got in trouble at school today 'cause we were play fightin' like grown-ups and I called him a sorry son of a bitch and he told me to shut the hell up."

It takes everything I have in me not to laugh. "Wow, yeah, I can see how that would get you in trouble. Probably shouldn't say grown-up words like that anymore at school."

Before they can say anything, a lady comes walking up with a buggy. "You two, let's go." I glance at the buggy and see beer, cigarettes and some TV dinners.

I guess I should introduce myself since this lady isn't even going to ask her children who they're talking to. I raise my head and put my hand out. "Hi, I'm Elaine—" Before I can finish I see her face, like really see it. "Brandi?"

She finally looks at me. "Well, hell, Elaine. I didn't know you had a kid, too."

Man, she looks bad. Like she's on something. "Yeah, I guess he and the twins are in the same class."

"Well, that's good. What are you doing now?"

I smile, "I'm a nurse at Memorial."

"Where you livin'?"

Ugh. "For the time being we're staying at my mom and dad's. I'm getting divorced, so I'm there, but they help with Lox, so it works out." I don't say my husband ran off in the middle of the night after I caught him screwing a woman on our couch and I told him I was pregnant. I also don't add in that I'm having trouble getting divorced because we can't find the bastard.

"Oh yeah, I forgot you got married to that college guy."

"Yeah, it didn't work out so well. He hasn't been in the picture since before Lox was born. It's proven hard to get the divorce finalized."

She leans into me. "Men are useless. The boys' daddy died working as a long haul driver. He died a few months ago and left me a little bit of life insurance, but that was just enough to bury him. I'm working at the truck stop waiting tables. So my momma is helping me raise the boys. They're hellions."

I nod, realizing that this girl is definitely not the girl who grew up as my best friend. It also occurs to me that waiting tables may not be the only thing she's doing for money at the truck stop.

"It was good to see you, but I need to go pick up a couple of things for Momma. I've got to go into work in a little bit."

"All right, girl, well it was good to see ya! We need to hang out sometime."

I give her what I hope looks like a genuine smile. "Yeah, for sure." I take in the state of the boys, their clothes, how dirty they are, how one of them acts starved for attention, while the other one is so distant. I may regret this but, "Hey, maybe one night when I'm going to be off and you're working, the boys can come stay with Lox."

Her face lights up. "Yeah, that'd be great. I'll give you a call. Your parents still got the same number?"

I nod. "Sure do."

"Good, we'll do that then."

Walking away, my heart sinks. She looks like hell and those boys are suffering for it.

Sure enough, it only takes a couple of weeks before she calls me with an emergency, needing the twins to stay with me.

Since then they've been with us at least four or five nights a week. She says her mom is sick and can't help her right now. According to my dad, Brandi has been in and out of trouble for the past few years. It may be two more mouths to feed but I love them. They've already grown on me and my parents. They call my parents Gran and Pop just like Lox. I've gotten them to clean up their language and even gotten Huck where he'll talk to me.

A good thing is I was told today that I got the open position on day shift at the hospital ER so I can spend even more time with them. This also means a little bit of a pay raise and with the money I've been saving living with mom and dad for the past five years, I have enough to make a down payment on a house.

It hasn't been easy to rebuild my life with a kid, but I'm getting there.

I found a little three-bedroom ranch-style house a few streets over from my parents, so that will make it convenient and it's in my price range. I've applied for all of the first-time homeowner programs and assistance programs and finally got somewhere. My dad keeps begging me to wait until my divorce is finalized so Jeff can't come in and claim my house, but my attorney says it's not likely he will. That I have documentation of when he left and so much more against him. With me having three boys, more and more we need our own space. I'm to the point I'd almost rather her just give them to me to take care of and stop dropping in and out of their lives. I talked to her mom after she said she was sick and her mom said that she told Brandi she wouldn't keep the boys for her to go out of town with a truck driver she just met, so she lied and told me her mom was sick so she'd have someone to watch them. She's a piece of work. But I'm not here to criticize, I just want to keep the boys happy, healthy, and clean.

A week into my new shift I'm told we have some students coming in from UF. They're all in pre-med classes, so this should be great. They're going to think they know more than someone like me who has been doing this job for five years, just because they're going to have the initials DR in front of their name eventually.

"Elaine, the students are here, is there any way you can show them around for a second while I get the conference room ready?" the ER doctor asks me.

"Yes, sir." I follow him down the hall to the desk, he points them out and walks to the conference room.

"Hey, everyone, I'm Elaine Storm, I'm a RN here and have been for five years. If you'll come with me, I'll do my best to show you some of the ins and outs of the ER while Dr. Shaw gets the room ready for you guys."

After a quick tour, the doctor lets me know that the room is ready and one of the students stops on the way in the door. "Your name is Elaine Storm?"

I nod, "Yes and you are?"

He grins a little. "I'm John Beck, we have a mutual friend I believe."

"Okay?" This is a little weird.

"Vance DeMarco?"

Okay, that's a little shock, I haven't thought about him for a little while. Well, that's a lie, I think about what might have been every day, but I try not to allow it. "Yes, he and I were friends years ago. I haven't talked to him in a long time." Then it hits me, I do remember him. "Oh yeah, you were his battle buddy when he went to boot camp."

He nods. "Yeah, I was. Look, I need to go in here, but afterward can I talk to you for a minute? Maybe have some coffee?"

Okay, this is really getting weird. I know he's not dead or really hurt, my dad would've told me. Although, I know he doesn't send Dad letters as much anymore. I think a minute longer. "Okay, we can grab a coffee in the cafeteria, just let me know when you finish."

He nods. "Great."

A few hours later, I'm sitting across from a man I haven't seen in almost ten years. "So, what did you want to talk about?"

"I know your dad used to keep in contact with Marco, does he still?"

"I'm not sure. Why?"

"Well, he's had a rough time the past few years and if your dad could talk him through some stuff, I think he may be the only person he'd listen to."

"Is he okay? Has he been hurt? Last time I knew anything, my dad was listed as his emergency contact."

"Not physically hurt, but I think mentally. The spiral started when your dad sent him a picture right after your son was born." My hand flies to my mouth and then I clear my throat.

"I, um, didn't know Dad did that."

"Yeah, then he got mixed up with the wrong woman and it ended up getting his ass transferred to a base on the other side of the world for a little bit. I'm worried about him. He normally stays in contact with me, but the last few times I've talked with him, he's been off. I was wondering if I gave you his number, do you think maybe your dad would call him? He could always seem to talk to him, get him out of his own head." I can tell he's really having an inner battle asking me to do this.

"You know he broke up with me, right? I never wanted to break up with him. I would've followed him to the end of the Earth back then."

He nods. "Yeah, I know. I also know you're married and have a kid."

"I'm in the middle of a divorce from a husband who hasn't been in the picture for five years and yes, I have a five-year-old son. He's my world. He told me to move on and I did after a while, but it was the worst mistake in my life. Even though I wouldn't change it, because I wouldn't have my son." I sigh, "But I will pass the message along to my dad."

"Thank you. I know this is all just a lot, but seeing you today was like, I don't know, a sign or something."

I wave my hand, "Okay, enough about that. So, you're pre-med?"

"Yes and no, I'm going to school to be a chiropractor, but I have to pretty much take all of the same classes as the regular pre-med students. This is my last semester, though, before I enter the doctorate program."

"Sounds interesting." Just then my pager goes off. "Well, I'm sorry to cut this short, but I have to go. Leave the number at the desk for me and I'll give it to Dad."

He stands up, tossing his empty cup in the garbage. "Thanks and, Elaine, if it means anything, I think he regretted his decision every day after he left here."

I just nod before I run back to the ER. I can't think about that. I've cried too many tears over it in the past.

PART II

CHAPTER 12

MARCO

November 2000

Looking in my rearview mirror, the gates to Camp Lejeune get smaller and smaller. I've spent the last thirteen years of my life dedicated to the Corps. Even after that asshole Haas made my life a living hell. I haven't laid eyes on him or Rosalinda in almost nine years. The night of the ball she said she was leaving for two weeks. By the time that two weeks was over with, I was on a ship. He stopped by my place alone and made sure I knew, though, that if I tried to make contact with her again, I'd suffer and she'd suffer.

I'll never forget the last conversation we had.

I called him a dickless bastard and asked why with all the other women he was fucking he wouldn't let her go. He laughed and said, "Because, I don't have to, I wear the brass here. I found her in some shithole town in a trailer park and gave her the life she has today. She owes me, I am a mother fucking colonel and no lowly, sniveling, lovesick fucking sergeant is going to take what I own." He shook his head. "You're an excellent Marine, that's why I'm just relocating you. Just remember, if you try to get in touch with her, just know her life can be a lot worse. I've never laid my hands on her; when I found out about you, I wanted to, but I didn't. I can, though, and not one soul on this base will protect her. What officers do in their home is no one else's business. I can also put you in the most uncomfortable, unsafe places known to man. Don't fuck with me."

"Why don't you quit being a pussy and take off the rank and we'll see who the real man here is? You talk all this shit, how you could hurt her, make her life bad, you hide behind that brass. I bet you've never even been in a fight before. So, Colonel, let's see what you're made of and we'll leave it all here," I barked.

He cracked his neck and nodded, "Sure, why not? I'd love to kick the ass of the man who fucked my wife. You're out of here in forty-eight hours anyway and hopefully the only way you'll come back is in a—" Before he could finish the sentence I punched him in the face. By the time we finished, my apartment was a wreck and his face looked like he got hit by a truck.

"You gonna call the MPs now, let them know you got your ass handed to you by an enlisted?" I asked, wiping my lip from the couple of hits he got in.

He shook his head, wiping his bloody nose with his sleeve. "Nope, I can think of more things to do than that to you. There's more I can take from you than you'll ever know."

I never got the opportunity to respond before he walked out my door.

I don't have an exact plan right now. I've got opportunities. As a matter of fact, after that fight, I went to a bar to drown myself in whiskey and ran up on a man I've come to consider a friend. He's kept in contact, offered me a place in the Hellions MC and a pseudo family time and time again. I'm just not sure I'm ready to lock myself down with the Hellions and Roundman yet. Staying in North Carolina isn't something I've really considered. I kind of want to put as much distance as I can between me and this state.

I have quite a bit in savings. Since I've had a steady income, but very few expenses, I've been able to put away. The only thing I've bought is this car and the few times I've paid rent. I never really spent money. So, I've got time. I'll get a job somewhere, though; I like having my savings after how I grew up. My parents' shitty trailer and working dead-end jobs to barely pay bills—I just can't do it.

I know I'm planning to go south, but not to my hometown. Beck has been trying to talk me into moving home, he's partner in a chiropractor clinic. He says I should come and open a gym to train fighters or open a firearms range, that the little town outside of Gainesville that I'm from is growing, but I just can't. I said I would never go back there.

Elaine is there, I know from when I went off the rails a few years ago and her dad called me to get my head back on straight that she's divorced, or should be by now. That the guy was a piece of shit. I just can't face her. Call me a coward, a pussy, whatever you want, but that woman could still ruin me. It's taken me all of these years to realize that yes, I loved Rosalinda, but she was never Elaine.

Turning up the radio, I jam out to my Offspring CD as I drive. Miles go by and I change the CD a few times. My mind goes through memories like a slide show. Years of memories.

My new cell phone starts ringing, jarring me from my thoughts, and I know it can only be one person, Beck. He's the only person who has my number. Hell, I'm still getting used to it, I know I'll have to get a local number wherever I go. I've never had a need for one until now. I hit the green phone key. "Hello."

"Hey, man, how's the ride going?" His voice sounds like he's holding something back.

"It's fine, man, but if this isn't really important, can I call you back? I didn't get a plan with many minutes and we're roaming right now so this is burning them up. I can call you back after nineteen hundred, though."

"Well," he pauses, "Hugh Loxley had a stroke today."

I almost hit the brakes on the interstate. "What?"

"Yeah, he's in ICU at Memorial. I figured since you don't really have a plan right now, you may wanna come on down and check on him. I think he'd like to see you."

I shake my head. "Shit." I let out a sigh, the man has done so much for me. He's been my sounding board, and he's shown me the kind of man I want to be one day. I know he's never told her that we keep in touch, just like I asked, he kept his word. Hell, he's been more of a father to me than the shitty biological one I had.

"Marco, you still there or did the call drop?"

"I'm here. Yeah, I'll come see him. You gotta couch I can crash on for a day or two?"

"Yeah, man. I think he's gonna be okay. I went by today and Elaine's holding it together, but Mrs. Loxley is not doing so great."

"All right, man. Don't say anything about me coming in. Okay?"

I hear him laugh. "Roger, man. Call me when you get closer and I'll give you my address."

"I'm still at least five hours from Gainesville so it'll be a little bit."

"Talk soon, Marco."

So my plan is to visit Hugh and make sure he's going to be okay, visit for a day or so with Beck and then get the hell out of there. Hopefully, I can miss Elaine altogether.

~*~

When I called for Beck's address earlier, he also gave me the visiting hours at the hospital, so I decided go ahead and swing by there on my way in. He promised me that Elaine should be at home with her kid because of him having school tomorrow.

Riding the elevator up to the fifth floor, my stomach feels like I may puke. I haven't seen this man since the day before I broke his daughter's heart thirteen years ago. Yeah, I've kept in touch with him and I know he cares for me, but seeing me in person, not so sure about it.

As I step off the elevator, my eyes land directly on her. She's talking to someone at the nurses' station, holding a little boy's hand. I can tell by her body language that she's heading for the elevator so like the pussy I am, I step into a bathroom and peek out the door until I see her leave.

Taking a deep breath, I go back out into the hallway and stop at the nurses' station to see about getting in to see him.

"I'm here to see Hugh Loxley."

She looks at the clock. I know visiting time is almost over, but I'm going to try to see him. I give her a grin. "I know I'm cutting it close, but I just drove all the way here from Camp Lejeune to see him." Small lie.

Her eyes go big. "Oh my goodness. I'll buzz you in, through that door." She points. "Once you get in, he's in room fourteen. It's on the right."

I look at her badge. "Thanks, Mandy."

She smiles. "No problem."

Making my way through the heavy doors and then down the tile hall, I stop outside of the room, mentally preparing myself. Just as I'm about to go in, Mrs. Loxley steps out, almost running into me.

"Oh, excuse…" Before she can finish her hands fly to her mouth. "Oh my lord, Hugh, look who it is." She wraps her arms around me. "It's so good to see you, sweetheart." She pulls my face to her and kisses my cheek. "You're just…well this is…oh gosh, listen to me, I can't even make a sentence," she says, shaking her head. Her hair is still dark with a few gray hairs scattered throughout. Overall, though, she still looks like that same loving woman who sent me care packages and letters when I was in boot camp. The woman who wanted to make sure that I knew I was loved even if it wasn't by my own parents. My heart breaks a little realizing how much I've missed these people.

"Nellie." It comes out a little slurred. He motions with one hand, "L-let h-im c-come in, h-he l-ooks t-tired." Hugh looks older, his hair is mostly gray now, and he looks tired. It's hard seeing a man that I've viewed as larger than life for all of these years looking so frail, but I know him, he's not going to let it beat him. He's hooked up to all kinds of monitors and they beep quietly at a steady rhythm.

"Oh yes, I'm sorry, this is just such a big surprise. You just missed Elaine," she says with a smile, I can see a few more lines in her face showing her age a little more.

"Man, that's too bad," I say, hoping that they can't tell I'm lying.

"Well, sit down and visit." She motions to the chair beside Hugh, "I'm gonna go ahead and go home. I was headed out when you came in."

I think about her walking out to the parking lot alone. "Do you want me to walk you down?"

"No, sweetie. Elaine already spoke with Willie, the security guard. He'll walk me out to my car." Her smile never leaves her face.

"Okay, if you're sure?" I ask, glancing out in the hallway like I'm scared Elaine will show back up any minute.

"Yes, honey. You have a nice visit and I expect to see you again before you leave." With that she walks out the door.

I take a seat beside his bed and he looks over at me. "So, are you around for good or on leave?" It's slow and a little garbled, but I understand him.

"Well, I'm out, but I don't think I'm staying here. I just never wanted to come back here." I keep my eyes on the TV hanging from the wall, trying to avoid his eyes. I just can't look him in the eyes right now and tell him how seeing all of them has gut-punched me and in a matter of ten minutes made me question all of my decisions over the past thirteen years.

"I understand," he mumbles. "Who told you?"

He's talking about him. "Beck called me. I was on my way south. I don't really even know where I was going, but he called and so I came here to check on you, old man." I try to lighten the mood with a laugh, turning my face back to him.

He mutters, "Things happen for a reason."

I nod in agreement. "I guess so." Looking up at the clock, I see it's been several minutes since I begged to get in here, so I better not push it. "I'm gonna go crash at Beck's," I point to the clock, "I better not push my luck. I'll be back by tomorrow, before I leave town."

He clears his throat and tries to move his right hand, but it's hard for him. I reach over and grab it in a handshake to help him. "Good to see you," he slurs.

"You, too, old man. I'll catch you tomorrow, get some rest."

I hear him try to say, "You, too."

~*~

It takes me fifteen minutes to get to Beck's place, he's all pumped up to introduce me to this woman he's planning to get engaged to, Gloria.

I grab a duffle with clothes and knock on the door. A petite, brunette girl answers the door. "You're not the pizza guy."

I chuckle. "Nope. Never been a pizza guy."

She points to my duffle. "So that narrows it down to hobo passing through town or Vance DeMarco," she replies, placing a hand on the door frame. "So, tell me the answer."

I grin, "Well, I guess you could say I'm a little bit of both."

She breaks into a full-blown laugh, "Nice to finally meet you, Marco, I'm Gloria."

"Nice to meet you, too. I hear a lot of good things about you. My buddy seems pretty smitten."

I hear someone moving behind her. "Oh damn it, Marco, I was playing it all aloof and shit."

She turns around to him, "Hate to tell you, babe, but you suck at it."

"Well, are you going to make him sleep on the porch or let him in, baby?" Beck asks.

She steps back, grinning, "Well, honestly I was kinda hoping the pizza guy would show up while I had the door open."

I step inside and Beck laughs at her while handing me a beer. "Babe, just go sit down. I'll get the door when he gets here."

I point to Gloria. "I like her."

He snickers, "Yeah, she's great. I picked her up at the Wal-Mart one day when I was buying condoms!" he says loud enough for her to hear.

We walk on in and I hear her from the kitchen. "Yeah, he was buying small ones and I felt bad for him. So, I took a chance, turns out he's a doctor and the money is good."

I burst out laughing, "Damn, I really like her, she busts your balls."

We sit down on his couch and he leans back. "Yeah, she's great. Really great."

"So, where did you meet her?" I say, taking a sip from my beer.

He looks over at me. "She's my partner's daughter," he replies before taking a long sip from his bottle.

I start laughing. "How in the hell did that happen?"

He shakes his head, "Not planned, that's for damn sure. I'm positive her dad is regretting our business contract at this moment."

"Risky, but who the fuck am I to say anything?"

Seriously, who am I to lecture someone on risky relationships?

CHAPTER 13

ELAINE

When my phone rang at almost ten o'clock last night, I was scared something was wrong. Depending how you look at it, well, it could be. As my mother gushed on the phone about how handsome Vance was, I just shook my head and vowed to kill Beck. I really can't complain too much, though; I mean she said Daddy was thrilled to see him. Apparently, he showed up right after I left last night. She said he was planning to come back today, so I've decided to help them by doing some healthy grocery shopping. Daddy will probably go home in a few days and just have a therapist coming out to the house. So, I'm going to make sure the house is stocked with good foods. Also, this means I can avoid the hospital.

Feeling the weight of something falling in the buggy, I look up to see Sly putting a case of beer in it. "Sly, what are you doing?" I say through my teeth, embarrassed that someone is watching.

"That's Pop's beer. He said the stuff at the hospital was shit, so I figured he'd really want his beer when he got home." He smiles.

I shake my head, this just keeps getting better and better. One day this kid is going to be a lady killer. "Okay, while that is a nice thought, there are a few problems. Number one, you don't need to be picking up beer. Number two, Pop isn't going to be able to have beer. Number three, what have I said about cussing?"

His smile turns down a little. "Sorry about saying shit."

I can't help but laugh and ruffle his hair. "It's okay." The boys are pretty much with me all the time now. Brandi's in a rehab facility *again* and her mom just can't handle them. I wish she would just sign them over to me, she won't though because that means her check gets cut. I worry to death when they are with her, they tell me about the men that come in and out of there. Hell, a few years ago she just up and disappeared for like two damn months. Not a word to her mother or me. How in the hell was I ever friends with her?

A small crash makes me run to the end of the aisle and find Lox and Huck standing in the middle of several boxes of cereal. "Guys, what happened?"

Lox shakes his head. "I swear, Mom, I just grabbed one box and they fell."

"Boys, you have to be careful." I look at the boxes. "Guys, Pop doesn't need Fruit Rings anyway." I start picking them up and trying to restack them.

Huck pipes in, "But we're out at home."

"Holy moly, guys, I just bought two boxes a couple of days ago."

"We're growing, Mom," Sly answers, placing two boxes in the buggy.

"Sounds pretty logical to me," a male voice says behind me.

I turn around and face the past. Damn, he's like wine, he only gets better with age. Muscles on muscles. I think my panties just went up in flames. *Calm down, Elaine,* I tell myself. "Hey, Vance, I heard you were in town."

"Yeah, just for a few days," he replies.

I nod and Huck steps in front of me. "Who are you?" Oh, the protector in the bunch, I swear he's the one who would take on a lion for me.

Vance looks around almost nervous looking. "I'm an old friend, your mom," he glances at me confused, "and I went to school together."

I tug Lox over to me. "Vance, this is my son, Lox." I put my hands on top of Huck and Sly's heads. "These two rascals are my chosen kids. Huck and Sly. They're Lox's best friends and Brandi's kids."

He sticks his hand out to the boys and shakes each one of their hands. "You guys can call me Marco."

Sly looks him up and down, "Man, you're one big hammer knocker." I snort and he gives a deep laugh.

"Yeah, I guess I am. Comes with the job," he replies, shrugging.

"Well, what are you, like some kind of body builder or something?" Sly keeps prying.

He shakes his head. "No, I'm a Marine."

Sly's eyes get really big. "Wow, so you're badass, huh?"

"Sly, what have I told you about those words?" I warn, trying to stifle my laugh. I know I shouldn't but the boys just have this charm.

He sighs. "Sorry, that was a bad word for me to say."

I tip my head to the side. "Now, since this is twice in the grocery store, what are you going to do when we get home?"

His shoulders slump. "Write some sentences."

I nod. "Yes. Now, no more questions."

Vance turns his attention back to me. "Interesting group you have here."

I sigh, shaking my head. "Oh yeah, it's never dull. I'll tell you that."

"Well, I went by and saw your dad this morning. He seems to be doing well. Your mom said he may get to come home in a few days."

"Yeah, I'm here trying to pick up some healthy options for him and apparently a few things for my own house," I respond, motioning to the buggy.

He laughs, "I'm sure Hugh is going to *love* that."

I roll my eyes. "For sure." Sarcasm drips from his tone.

"Well, I just came out to grab some steaks for Beck and me to grill tonight," he says, motioning to his buggy.

This is so awkward. I nod, "So you're staying with Beck? Have you met Gloria?"

He laughs, "Yeah, last night. She's hilarious. Gives Beck sh—crap. It's great. So you've met her?"

"Yeah, actually I ran into them here in the store one day. Small town life at its finest. He introduced us, she works as a physical therapist at the same hospital I work at. So we have lunch sometimes."

"That's great. He seems head over heels."

I laugh, "They're good for each other." I feel a tugging on my arm.

"Mom, I gotta go pee," Lox says.

"Okay, the three of you go. You know the rules about talking to people. I'll wait for you outside the door." I start walking the few feet down to the bathrooms.

Once the boys are all inside, he motions to the bathroom. "So, Brandi's kids?" he questions.

I sigh, "Yeah, she's a mess. She's trying rehab again. I have them more than she does. Her mom helps her, but the boys are just too much for her. I love them, so to me they're mine."

"Wow. That's big."

I don't really know what to say to him. The boys, all of them, are my heart. They are my life. "So, you just home on leave?" I ask, trying to figure out how long my heart will be stuck in my throat.

"No, I'm officially out. Trying to decide what comes next. You know?"

"Sure." Before I can say anything else, three little boys come tearing out of the bathroom doors.

"Okay, can we go now?" Huck says, eyeing Vance.

I laugh at my little protector. "Yeah, guys, I think we've got enough for Gran and Pop." I look back over to Vance. "It was good to see you."

"You, too," he says with a small grin.

Casually, I stroll to the checkout while inside I want to make a beeline to the car. After we drop all of my parents' groceries off I decide to go ahead and take the boys by the hospital to visit my dad. Especially since I know that Vance has already been by, it seems like a perfect plan. Generally, you don't get to take kids of this age to the unit, but that's the great thing about me working there. I can pull strings.

When I pull up in the parking lot of the hospital, I turn around and look at the boys. "What are the rules here?"

They all say, "No running, no being loud, stay right with you and don't bother anyone."

I laugh and smile. "Okay, let's go."

Once we reach my dad's room, we walk inside. "Hey, Daddy, thought you might want a little company."

He gives me a lopsided smile. "Yep." He and my mom never treat the twins any different than Lox. It makes my heart so happy.

My mom comes out of the small bathroom. "Well, isn't this a surprise. I didn't know we'd get visits from so many handsome fellas today."

Each of the boys take turns hugging my parents.

"Mom, I went to the grocery store for you guys today since word from Daddy's doctor is he'll be sprung from this place in a couple of days."

Sly is sitting up in the bed with my dad. "She wouldn't let me get your beer, Pop. I told her you were tired of the shit here, but she just wouldn't listen, she just kept putting vegetables in the buggy."

My mom's mouth drops open and my dad laughs. I point my finger at him, "Sly, I told you about those words and I also explained to you why Pop can't have his beer.

Since you've already been assigned some sentences for your words, let's add another hundred to that."

My dad gives Sly a hug the best he can. "Thanks for trying to help," he mumbles.

"So you guys went to the grocery store?" my mom asks, trying to take some of the pressure off of my dad trying to talk.

They all nod. "Yeah, and Mom was talking *forever* to this guy named Marco," Lox says, rolling his eyes dramatically.

I roll my eyes just like my son and Mom gives me a look. "Yes, we ran into my old *friend* from school, Vance."

My mom smiles. "Oh, so you saw Vance? That's good. He looks great, doesn't he?"

I nod. "Yes, he looks like life is treating him okay."

Huck is standing there with his arms crossed looking like he just ate a lemon. "He talks too much."

My parents laugh, knowing that is not how someone would describe Vance. My mom rubs his shoulder. "Maybe he and Mom were just trying to catch up."

"Yeah, well, I don't like it," he mumbles. "We had stuff to do and he wasn't part of getting that done."

Lox shrugs, grabbing the remote. "He was pretty cool to me."

Sly giggles. "*I think he likes you. I think he wants to kiss you,*" he singsongs.

"Ugh, boys, chill out. We were just catching up. He won't even be in town long."

One can only hope, for the sake of my heart and my panties.

CHAPTER 14

MARCO

Putting the steaks in to marinate, I think about seeing her. I laugh at her wrangling those three boys. Her biological child seems quiet, but those twins are something, that's for sure. I hate that she's still cleaning up Brandi's messes. It was that way all through school. At least if she has those boys, they're in great hands. Her dad had mentioned once or twice on the phone that she had Brandi's kids, I just thought he meant for the weekend or something. Not that she'd taken them on to fucking raise. In all the times I've talked to him or Beck, they've tried their best not to bring her up. They know for me, it's still a subject I don't stomach well.

"So, how was the grocery store? Just like you remembered?" Beck asks, walking in the kitchen popping a chip in his mouth.

"Nope, they moved the chip aisle," I say, dripping sarcasm. "I did, however, run into exactly who I was trying to avoid."

He starts laughing. "Ha, man, I told you avoiding crap wouldn't work out."

I wave him off, "Yeah, yeah, fuck you."

"So?"

"So what?"

"So did you run to each other and collapse into a bin of chips? Was there background music? Was LeAnn Rimes in the background singing 'How Do I Live...'" I toss a rag at him to get him to shut up.

I grab a beer from the fridge. "No, asshole. She was shopping for her parents with three kids."

He nods. "Yeah, her kid and Brandi's twins."

"From what all she said I take it Brandi is still a fucking mess."

He nods. "I didn't know her in high school like you guys, but I know those boys are better with Elaine."

"Oh yeah, not a doubt in my mind," I reply before taking a sip from my beer.

He grabs one for himself. "So for real, how did it go?"

"We only spoke for a couple of minutes, I think she was just as uncomfortable as me. Those kids, though, man, her son is quiet, one of the twins is wide open and the other is like dead serious. I've literally seen that look in the eyes of people who've trained me."

He grabs the bag of chips and motions for me to follow him to the patio. "Elaine has really taken care of herself. I mean yeah, her parents have been her backup, but she busted her ass. Gloria loves her."

"Yeah, she told me they do lunch and shit."

The suspense is killing me for the question I really want to ask. "So what about her ex? Is he ever around?"

He shakes his head. "No, hell, last account I had they couldn't even find the mother fucker so she could officially divorce him. I almost wish the son of a bitch would show up so I could kick his ass."

Are you fucking kidding me? "So no one has any leads on him?"

"Nope, he left the day she found out she was pregnant with Lox."

I stand up and go grab another beer from the fridge. I left her here so she would have a better life, so she could find a great man. This guy shit all over that. I wanted her to have the house, the kids and a husband that stood by her. I'm sure her life is great in a way, but not the great I wanted for her. She's had to do it mostly on her own and with extra kids to boot. If that guy walked up in front of me right now, I'd probably put him in the ground. The fucker runs off and she can't even officially get him out of her life, what kind of fucked up shit head does that? I'm gonna go talk to Hugh about this before I leave. I know Hugh, he has to have found something by now and if he has, I'm going to do my best to end this for her.

~*~

Here I am on another road trip. After talking with Hugh, he did have a few leads, but couldn't get very far without cause. Good thing for me with all of my years with the military, I have friends that owe me favors. Turns out he didn't go very far, he's down in Homestead. He's not employed, go figure, so that's what made it more difficult to find him. I managed to get ahold of the divorce papers, I don't know how Hugh got them and I'm not asking. I just told him not to tell her what I was doing.

A few hours later, I'm pulling up in front of a small house in a nice neighborhood. Grabbing the manila envelope, I walk up to the door and knock. A short blonde opens the door. "Can I help you?"

"Yes, I'm looking for Jeffery Storm."

"He's here. Hold on and I'll get him."

She turns and yells, "Jeff, honey, there is a man at the door to see you."

"Who is it? I'm busy on the computer."

That pisses me off because you can tell he's ran this woman to death, too. He's probably running up their phone bill with damn internet charges. Fuck him. "Tell him that it has to do with his wife and child," I grit out.

I can tell from her face she's shocked. She spins around and storms out of the foyer, leaving the front door open. "You son of a bitch. He's here about your WIFE AND CHILD! Go see what he needs and then pack your shit and get the fuck out of my house! I'm tired of supporting your good for nothing ass."

"I don't have a wife or a child, this is just a misunderstanding, honey. Let me go find out about it," I hear him trying to play her.

I step to the side of the door so he can't see me head on. He steps out the door to see who is here, I catch him by the throat and slam him into the wall. "You may not remember me, we met briefly, but I've got some papers here for you to sign, then you can go back to being the sorry piece of shit you are. Although, I'm gonna make sure this lady knows the truth."

He shakes his head. "Oh, I know who you are. I'm not sure who was more in love with you, Elaine or her parents. All I heard about was how wonderful you were, there were pictures of you and her up all around her parents' house. Hell, they never even put up our wedding photo. What, now you need her to get divorced so you can marry her?"

I shake my head. "This has nothing to do with me. It has to do with you being a drain on society. Living off of unsuspecting women. Being a deadbeat dad."

"I told her to get rid of the damn kid," he growls.

That's where my restraint ends, I draw back and punch him in the face. "If I wouldn't have to live with it, I'd kill your ass and drop you in the Everglades, let the gators eat you."

"What do you want? I don't have money."

"She's doing fine on her own, she doesn't need your money, or lack thereof. She just wants you to sign these papers. Now, she could go to the courts, show them your address and get you saddled with all of the back child support you owe. Or you could just sign these papers granting her a divorce and signing away your rights to her child."

He huffs out a breath, "Fine. Give me the damn papers."

I put my hand up. "Wait, let's take these in to the table so you have something to write on. Oh, and we need another witness."

Laughing, I stop at the nearest Office Depot to get the papers sent to Hugh. He's going to say a friend took care of it for him. I told him I wanted to do this for her, but I can't let her know.

I tell you what, though, watching that woman toss all of his clothes out into the yard and kick him in the balls after she signed as a witness was awesome. Now, I'm getting up with a buddy in Miami while I try to figure out what I want to do next.

~*~

January 2003

I hold the phone to my ear and listen to Beck ramble. "Man, I'm telling you, you should come up here and open a gym like you've been working at down there."

"Beck, I don't want to clean out my savings to open a gym." I try to explain my concern for the millionth time.

"I'll invest in it," he throws out there.

"Man, you're getting married and have a kid on the way." Hell, he'd been saying he was going to propose ever since he met her. He waited until a year ago, I think that was more to make his partner/soon-to-be father-in-law happy. Her mother has been planning a huge ass wedding, but they found out a month ago that they have a baby on the way.

I hear him growl. "It's been two years since you've been here. My business is booming, I have money to invest and I actually need to invest some of it in something. The wedding my in-laws insisted on paying for, traditional bullshit, and as far as the kid we'll be fine. Gloria and I both do very well." I hear him shuffle some papers. "All I'm saying is when you come up for the wedding in two weeks, I have some paperwork to show you. I think you could make a damn good business here and quit making money for other people."

I'm walking in the current place I'm working that I actually have grown to hate. The mentality they breed here is toxic. "Fine, we'll talk when I get there."

"Good," is all he says before he hangs up.

For the first time in sixteen years, I actually think about moving home and it doesn't make my stomach turn.

CHAPTER 15

ELAINE

March 2003

"Ms. Storm, I suppose you're here for the Webb twins along with your own son?" Principal Hastings says in a curt voice.

I look at him. "Brandi didn't answer?"

He shakes his head. "No." Of course she didn't, she's off with some damn trucker again. Shit like this is why I've been going through the foster parenting courses. If the school keeps trying to get ahold of her and she won't answer and it's always me, they'll eventually contact protective services. If this guy wasn't such a douchebag he would've already called them.

"Then yes, I'm here for them, too." I follow him in his office and see the three boys lined up in a set of chairs and another three boys lined up on the other side. I can tell they've all been fighting.

I stand in front of my three. "So, boys, care to tell me why I had to take off work to come here?"

"Ms. Storm, we'll wait until the other parents get here to get to the bottom of this, they should be here within the hour."

I look at him like he's lost his mind. "Within the hour? I'm sorry, that won't work. I took my lunch hour to come here. I'm going back to work, so let's get to the bottom of this now. I rushed over here as quick as I could. If I would've known we were wasting time, I would've waited longer."

He gives me a stern look. "Ms. Storm, we need to wait on the other families to get here. Marcus's mother is very upset."

Lord help me, I hate that woman. She looks down her nose at everyone at this school because she's married to a plastic surgeon, he's done a lot of work on her, and she's teaching her kid to be an asshole, just like the two of them. "I suppose she's who we're waiting the hour for?"

"Yes, she had an appointment in Gainesville," he replies.

I put my hand up to stop him. "I'm not waiting for her to finish getting her nails done. Some of us have work to do." I turn my attention to my boys. "Loxley Michael Storm, tell me what happened right now."

"They were talking smack about the twins, kept getting in their faces, so Huck popped Marcus in the face and then it all just went downhill."

"That's not true!" one of the boys from the other side yells.

I look at Huck, "What did he say?"

Huck looks down at the floor. "Now, Huck."

Sly butts in, "Marcus is pissed because Missy asked Huck to the dance and not him. He called us the thrown away kids and said that our own mother didn't even want us, then said she was a whore. Said that Missy only asked Huck as a joke." He glares around me to the other boys, "Which is crap because the girl has been following him around for weeks practically drooling."

I turn back to the boy in question and he won't look up. "Ms. Storm," the principal interrupts again, "it doesn't matter who said what, we have a zero-tolerance policy for fighting, so everyone who threw a punch will be suspended for five days."

I blow out a long breath, "Fine, then why didn't you just say that? If they're all guilty no matter what then why are you wasting time?" I look at my three boys. "Did you guys hit them?"

"Yes," they all say in unison.

I throw my hands up. "Okay, then let's go. Looks like five days I gotta sort out."

"Ms. Storm," he says, following me out, "we need to get to the bottom of this." I can tell he's all about pacifying Marcus's mom. Yes, she has some friends on the school board, but what he doesn't realize is I do, too. I helped save the superintendent's wife after a bad car crash. They still keep in touch with me. Hell, I get a fruit basket on my birthday and a gift card at Christmas. All I have to do is make a call. And for my boys, I will make every call necessary.

I spin around and put my finger in his face. "What's the point? You've already said if they passed a lick they get suspended. I'm not going to listen to the way you or miss prissy pants are going to talk to those boys." I lean in close and whisper, "But if I find out those other three are back before the five days are up, the school board will know about it and you'll start to figure out that just because I don't throw around who I know like those kids' parents do...I do know people." I turn my attention back to the boys. "Let's go."

Once we reach my car and everyone is buckled in, Sly laughs. "Dang, Mom, you gave it to him in there."

I turn around in my seat. "Sly, I am very upset with all of you right now. I was not kidding about this being my lunch time. I understand Huck had enough and do I like Marcus or his mom? No, but a free for all wasn't the way to correct it. Now, I have to stop and get gas, then I'm dropping you boys off at Gran and Pop's." Since my dad retired they travel, but luckily they're home right now. However, they leave in the morning for another trip.

Just before I pull into the gas station, I look up in the mirror to see three sad faces. I'm not saying anything else right now, I'm too worked up.

While I'm standing there pumping the gas I stretch my neck back and forth, trying to relieve some tension. "Looks like you're having a stressful day."

Damn, I know that voice. Gloria told me he was back for good, but I hadn't had an encounter with him yet. The last time I saw him was at Beck and Gloria's wedding a couple of months ago, but I was only there for the ceremony and had to go cover a shift at the hospital. He's been over to see my parents but only a few times. "Yeah, you can say that. I just went and picked up three thirteen-year-olds for fighting. They get a nice five-day vacation from school. All expenses paid."

He nods. "Wow. They sound like they've turned into a handful."

"They have in some ways, but not in others. Today someone was talking trash to Huck and it started with them and ended with the three of them and three other boys and a zero-tolerance policy."

"Sounds like they have a lot of energy to run out."

"Yeah, I'm taking them to my parents now, I've got to figure out the next five days because my parents are leaving in the morning. I may have to beg them to stay."

He starts shaking his head. "Don't do that. I think I have something that may help you."

Really, he's going to help me? I know something I'd love for him to help me with, but I don't have time for that. *Damn it, Elaine, get it together.* "Why would you help me, Vance?" I can't help but ask because why would anyone want to take on three teenage boys?

He tips his head to the side and sighs, "Because I'm still in awe of you. You handle these three kids most of the time by yourself. Hugh keeps me posted on everyone. I know the boys being young teens right now can be a lot. You know I was a teen boy once." He laughs, "Let me help you."

"How can you help?" I ask, the gas pump has stopped and I'm putting my cap back on.

"I'm opening an MMA gym."

What in the hell is he thinking? I put my hand up. "No. Them learning to fight isn't going to stop them from fighting at school, it'll just make them better."

He shakes his head. "That's not what I'm offering. I'm still setting it up and I need some cleaning and painting done. I'm sure I've got enough to keep them busy for their five days."

"So just working, no fighting or learning to fight?"

He shakes his head. "No, even though I could argue my point about the fighting, I won't."

Have I lost my mind for considering letting him do this?

"Do you trust me, Lainey?" Fuck me.

I'm probably the biggest damn idiot in the world. It's not like I have a lot of options, though. "Okay, give me the address."

He hands me a card with the address on it. "Okay, I'll need to drop them there about seven, is that okay?"

He nods. "Yep, I'm normally there by six-thirty. I have a couple of guys that followed me up from Miami that are doing some training with what I've managed to set up."

"Okay, I'm trusting you, Vance," I say sternly in my mom voice because well, I'm a mom and it happens. "I'll see you in the morning."

"See you then," he says just before I get back in my car.

"What did he want?" Huck asks as we leave the parking lot. He's still so suspicious of people talking to me.

"You guys are going to work on your time off. Gran and Pop are leaving on a trip in the morning and I was upset that I was going to have to ask them to hold off because you three can't stay out of trouble. However, Vance has a business and needs some extra hands."

"Is he going to pay us?" Sly asks with a cocky tone.

"No, he's not. Consider this your community service for your crimes."

They all sigh in the back seat and grumble all the way to my parents'.

~*~

Pulling up in front of what looks like an abandoned warehouse, I shake my head. Fuck, maybe I should just use my vacation days. I'm not sure about this place.

The boys are looking around as we get out of the car. "Are you sure about this place, Mom?" Lox asks.

"He says it's still a work in progress," I explain.

A heavy metal door opens and I see him step out, shirtless and sweaty and panty-melting sexy. Damn it! "Hey, guys, Elaine, how's it going?"

The boys grumble and I give a half smile. "We're here. That's about all I've got right now."

"Well, come on in and see the place." He motions for us to follow.

Walking inside, I see a bunch of studded walls. There is a punching bag and some weights in one corner, but not much else. "Wow, yeah, I'd say you have *a little* that the boys can help you with."

He chuckles. "Yeah, okay, it's a lot, but on the plus side they'll get some lessons in construction while they're here. Life skills, you know? I promise, though, we'll be careful."

I've got to get out of here before I look like a damn idiot school girl. I look at the boys who are staring around the room. "Okay, Lox, Sly, Huck, you remember my friend Vance, you met him when Pop had his stroke?" They all nod. "Well, this is your community service for deciding that fighting was the best decision to make at school." I turn to Vance. "Sly and Huck haven't recently, but they try to pull a switcheroo sometimes. Huck has a small scar above his left eyebrow, so that is your dead giveaway. He doesn't like to talk to people, so don't take it personal, you can't shut Sly up most of the time and Lox is quiet but will answer anything you have to ask." The boys all stare at me. "Look, guys, I'm giving him the lowdown because no one has time for the games this week."

Vance laughs, "I got it, Lainey. Guys, you can call me Marco. The first thing we're going to do is pull up some old carpet over here." He points to an area of the room. "You guys look strong enough to help me with that." They all three nod and start walking that way.

"Oh, I almost forgot, here are their lunches. I wasn't sure what you'd do, so..." Why am I so nervous? "Anyway, here it is. There's an extra one in there for you."

He smiles. "Thanks. See you this afternoon. Have a good day."

Sitting in my car, I lean my head back. *I really hope I have a spare pair of panties in my locker because these are soaked.*

CHAPTER 16

MARCO

I watch as Lainey trots out to her car. "You can quit staring at her ass anytime now, jackass."

I spin around to see the one she told me was Huck, "First thing, watch your mouth, I know she doesn't allow you to talk that way. Second, I wasn't staring at her ass and if I was it would be my business." I clamp my hand on his shoulder sternly, "Let's go tear up some old carpet."

After I have all three of their attention, I motion to the corners. "Probably the easiest thing to do is use these utility knives and cut along one edge and start pulling. You can either all work on the same piece or each take a piece. I don't know who put carpet in here like this, but it's stupid."

Lox nods, "Okay, I think we can all do a section, that'll make it a little quicker."

"Has Hugh had you guys help with some stuff like this?"

They all nod and Huck speaks, "Yeah, we helped him redo the den last summer."

"I've been by since then. It looks good." I chuckle thinking about the ugly gold carpet that used to be in there. "At least it's not got that gold shag carpet anymore."

Sly laughs, "Yeah, that stuff was butt ugly, but Gran said she wasn't replacing it until we quit spillin' drinks everywhere."

I laugh out loud, "I can see her saying that."

"I've seen pictures of you with my mom, you looked a lot different, but it was you. You were more than just friends from school," Lox says quietly. He is observant.

I give a small nod. Huck tips his head to the side, studying me. "Are you the asshole who up and left when she got pregnant?"

This kid, damn. "No, I can promise you, if I was your dad, Lox, I'd be here." I turn back to Huck, "Give me twenty-five push-ups."

His eyes bulge out. "What?"

"I've told you about your mouth. Now, give me twenty-five."

"Are you some kind of drill sergeant or something?" Sly asks.

I shake my head. "No, but I am a former Marine Gunny Sergeant, which means I take kids a little older than you with smart ass mouths like yours and break them down and build them back up. I know it works because I was a kid they did that to. Now, I know Lainey doesn't like you talking like that, so from now on, you cuss in here, you give me twenty-five."

Huck drops to the floor and starts doing push-ups, or what apparently he thinks are push-ups. "Whoa. Who taught you to do push-ups like that?"

"Coach Reed," they answer.

"Well, I don't think he knows his ass from a whole in the ground." I motion to the floor as they laugh, "Drop down, all three of you. I'm going to teach you a proper push-up."

After a few minutes they understand, Lox and Sly get up while Huck counts out twenty-five push-ups. "All right, let's go tear out this carpet."

A few hours later, we've got most of the carpet up and carried out to the dumpster in the parking lot. "What next?" Sly asks, wiping his face with the bottom of his shirt.

I point to the floor, "Grab one of those pry bars and get those carpet tack strips up. Huck, you come with me."

Out of the three of them, I can tell he has the most aggression built up. I asked them a little while ago what happened at school that caused them to get suspended. Sly pretty much gave me an ear full while the other two just nodded or rolled their eyes. I walk past the old bathrooms and into a small room. I grab the sledge hammer off the floor and hand it to him. "Here, start tearing down that wall."

His eyes go wide. "Like knock the wall out?"

I nod. "Yeah, go to town. Picture that little asshole's face you got in a fight with. I need this wall torn down so I can expand that bathroom and add some showers."

He takes his first swing, knocking a hole in the wall and grins. "Feels good, huh?" I ask.

He nods. "Yeah, so what are you going to do here? Open up some workout place?"

"Kind of," I answer as he takes another swing. "I train MMA fighters. I'm going to do some training with amateur fighters."

"Wow, so people pay you to teach them to fight?"

"In a way, yes, but it's about much more than fighting. It's about control."

"Does that help people who get mad a lot?" He's talking about himself, I know.

Elaine is going to kill me. "Yes, sometimes it's the release people need." I motion to the door. "Now, I've got to go check on the other two. You keep tearing down the wall." I point to the big square shovel. "Then use that shovel to push it all into one pile."

He nods. "Okay." Before I make it all the way to the hall, I hear him say, "Thanks."

When we break for lunch a couple of hours later, he and both other boys pepper me with questions about the military and fighting.

As the day rocks on I wait for Elaine to get here. The boys are hard workers, I'll give them that. They might have mouths on them, but they're just thirteen-year-old boys, full of piss, vinegar and hormones. I know I shouldn't be thinking it, she's going to kill me, but I think a program like this would do these boys some good.

"So, what are we going to do tomorrow?" Lox asks.

"Well, my buddy Beck is supposed to come by and help me hang some new sheetrock tonight and help me get it mudded. You guys will probably help me sand tomorrow."

I hear the door open behind me and turn around. One of the fighters I've been working with stops in front of me. "Hey, man, looks like you've got a crew here to work with you."

"Yeah, they're finishing up for the day. Why don't you go work on the speed bag for a little bit?" I motion over to the small corner where I have things set up.

He nods and jogs over that way. "While we wait on your mom, get those big brooms and sweep across this area. I need to go get him started."

They all nod and walk over to the brooms. I go over and start sparring with my trainee, noticing that they are doing more watching than sweeping. When the door opens again, Elaine is walking through in her dark blue scrubs, with her hair in a sloppy bun, looking exhausted. "Take five," I tell my guy before heading over to her and the boys.

"They were good today. We ripped up some carpet, Huck helped me tear down a wall," I tell her, motioning around the room.

She motions to the corner where I was. "What was that?"

"Oh, that's one of the guys I'm training. He just got here about thirty minutes ago," I explain. "Can I talk to you in the office for a minute?" I motion toward the office.

She nods. "Yeah, sure." Confusion is showing on her face.

Once we enter the office, which is basically just an empty room with a cheap Wal-Mart desk for right now, I give her the full rundown of the day, from language to the questions they asked.

She shrugs, "Hmm, push-ups, I never thought of that." Then she gives a small snort. "I can't believe they asked if you were Lox's dad."

"Well, Huck is the hard hitter when it comes to the questions. Lox just asked about the pictures of me in your parents' house," I say with a laugh. "Oh and he said I looked different."

She laughs. "They can be very observant."

"Now, one of the reasons I asked you in here is I think part of what is going on with them is just built up tension and anger. I know talking with the twins today some, they are angry about the shit Brandi is pulling. They think the world of you, but they are hurt by her actions."

She nods. "Yeah, I know. I wish I knew a good counselor to take them to, but I just don't and they aren't on my insurance. Though it seems they've opened up to you quite a bit in a day."

Only standing a few feet from her, all I want to do is pull her into my arms and kiss her tired lips, but I can't do that so I shrug, "It's just a guy thing. They're good kids, just rough around the edges."

"I always worry that I'm screwing up with them." She sighs.

I shake my head. "Never, but I did want to ask you, I know you don't want them fighting."

She holds up her hand to stop me. "No."

"I'm not asking for them to fight, but I am asking if they can work out with the speed bag and heavy bag. I think it would help get some of the aggression out. You should've seen Huck today tearing out that wall, when he was done," I shake my head, "it was like he felt lighter. He was joking with the other two and laughing. I didn't even know the kid could laugh." I reach over and touch her shoulder, feeling a small shock in my hand. "I just want them to have an outlet."

She sighs. "Let me think about it."

"Okay, that's all I'm asking."

After we walk back out to the boys, I motion to the walls, "We'll have sheetrock to sand tomorrow so wear old clothes, guys."

They all three look at me and nod. "Yes, sir."

"Come on, boys, I've got roast in the crock pot."

Huck stops in front of me. "Thanks for letting me tear out that wall today, it was kinda cool."

I nod. "All right. No problem."

"I'll try not to cuss tomorrow," he says.

"You know what happens if you do."

He nods. "Yeah, well, thanks." He turns and walks out the door and I can see the amazement in Elaine's eyes.

~*~

"So you got through to the terrible trio a little bit today, huh?" Beck asks as we hang sheetrock.

"Yeah, I think so. I'm hoping Lainey will let me workout with them some. Especially Huck, that kid has this fierceness in his face. He's pissed off at the world. He needs an outlet. Lox is so damn quiet and Sly covers everything with humor." I sound like I'm trying to be a shrink to kids I hardly know. "I don't know why I'm acting like I really know these kids." I rub my hand down my face and take a sip from the beer I'm drinking.

"You don't, however, the Marines taught you to study people. You're right, about it all. I've never actually been introduced to the boys. I know them through stories. Elaine has her hands full, she's just trying to make it." He shrugs. "You know?" He grabs a piece of sheetrock, holding it up to be screwed in.

"Yeah, I do," I answer before putting a screw in the piece. "I wish I could fix it all for her."

He levels his eyes at me as I grab another screw. "You can't, and furthermore, she won't let you. Don't push her too much or she'll back away. I thought she was going to kill me when I told her you were moving back here. I actually think you're part of the reason she's never introduced me to them. I really think she didn't want to explain how she and I met each other. She was just as much for avoiding you as you were her."

"Some days, I wonder what it would've been like if I wouldn't have broken up with her, if she'd have come with me," I grumble.

"Well, you'll never know the answer to that, all I can tell you is to live in the now. Get back that friendship with her and work from there," he says, moving down to change his hold so I can put another screw in.

"Yeah, well, that's the thing. I know in my heart that I've never been able to be *just friends* with her."

He shakes his head. "Well, that may be all she's willing to give you."

I groan, putting the last screw in that piece of drywall.

Days like today, I wonder if moving back here was the smartest thing I've ever done or the dumbest.

CHAPTER 17

ELAINE

Walking in with the boys the last day of their suspension, I can see all of the work they've done. This place is starting to look great. I am extremely proud of them. I have to give it to Vance, he's gotten more out of these boys in a week than any teacher has ever gotten out of them, and not just the physical labor.

One thing about my kids, they can smell bullshit a mile away and Huck especially isn't afraid to call you on it. So the fact that they've warmed up to Vance speaks volumes. Lox has never been a real big talker, he's a great kid, just more quiet than the other two, which with Sly as a friend he doesn't have much time to talk. Since he's been here, he's been talking more. Asserting himself a little more when it comes to the twins speaking for him. Huck's been a different kid, too, more affectionate to me and seems a little lighter in spirit. Sly is still silly as all get out, but I came in a little early yesterday and watched the boys hitting the heavy bag and speed bag. The look on Sly's face was all seriousness when he was hitting it. There was a concentration there like I've never seen before. Watching him with them, I can really tell they look up to him.

True to his word, Vance hasn't said anything about training them to fight. I have to admit, though, after talking over the phone to my dad about the control and discipline it takes to train and watching the boys, if they were to ask me if they could train, I'd probably break and let them. As a matter of fact, they have asked me if they can still come by after they finish up today. Which makes me think that this was possibly one of the best decisions I've ever made as a parent.

I glance around at the grey walls trimmed in black, it's coming to life. Following the boys down the short hall to a big open room that now holds a black and red training ring, my heart flutters when I see a shirtless Vance sparring with the guy that was in here the other day.

His body has changed through the years, he's no longer a tall lanky kid, now he's got a sculpted chest and tattoos. Lord, tattoos. God, they are sexy, that one on his lower abdomen does things to me. Sweat running down his chest, all of that sets my lady parts on fire.

He glances our way and calls out to the guy to take a break. He grabs a towel and wipes his face and chest. Stepping out of the training ring, he slips a shirt on. "Well, if it isn't my favorite construction crew."

The boys run up and all give him a high five, I give him a smile. "Last day of suspension, get all of the free labor you can out of them."

"Ah, yes, last day on the chain gang," he says, rubbing over Sly's head.

I laugh, "For some reason I'm pretty sure you have helpers whenever you need them."

"Man, I haven't been tough enough if you guys are jonesing to come back for more," he says, giving Huck a little shove in the shoulder.

"Hey, can you get back in there with him? We wanna see you spar some more," Lox says.

He glances to me and I nod, "They're your work crew today, not mine."

He pulls the shirt back off and tips his head toward the ring, "You heard them, Gus, let's go."

They climb back in and start swapping punches, and then it gets a little more intense. I see Vance sweep his leg around and take the other guy's legs out from under him.

Huck stands next to me. "He's been working with Gus for a few years. He said he comes up here from Miami just to train with Marco."

I nod, "Wow, it's pretty impressive. You seem really happy here with Marco."

He clears his throat. "Yeah, I mean he's pretty cool. It's kinda nice to have a guy besides Pop to hang out with."

I'll be honest, I've never brought anyone into the boys' lives. I've been on a few dates over the years, but nothing that stuck because I was too busy raising three kids. Vance is the first real male influence they've had besides my dad and teachers. "Good, I'm glad."

"You guys aren't going to start dating or anything, are you?" he says with almost a panic in his eyes.

I shake my head. "No, sweetie, it's not like that for us anymore." It hasn't been in a long time, even if deep down I always wonder what if it was.

"Okay, because they would be really upset if you guys broke up or something and we couldn't come here anymore," he says, trying to be the strong guy and not show that he would care, too.

I put my arm around his shoulder and ruffle his hair. "I got you, kid. No dating for me."

He pulls away a little and looks me in the eyes. "I don't want you to be alone, Mom, you should date. Just not Marco, okay?"

I pull him back in and kiss his forehead. "Okay." I look at the other two and him, "I'm going to get to work, guys. Work hard today, last day of your sentence."

I get a chin lift from Vance and the boys all wave at me.

Once I get back to the front door, I glance around the lobby one more time and think about that boy standing in the hallway leaned back against a locker with the cigarette tucked behind his ear. How far he's come from that trailer park with shitty parents. I smile, it brings a warmth to my chest. I'm so proud of him, and I'm glad he's become important to the boys, which is just a couple of the reasons why I need to move on. Truly move on this time.

Even when Jeff was in the picture, Vance was still in the back of my mind. I tried, or I tell myself I did, but it wasn't easy with Jeff. I won't take the blame for all that occurred in my marriage to Jeff, but I will say maybe I could've been more present. Instead of trying to get over Vance when I clearly wasn't ready, I should've waited longer, then maybe I wouldn't have missed all of the signs. The signs that he was a worthless piece of shit. The back side of that, though, is that I wouldn't have that beautiful boy in there…well, all three of those beautiful boys.

Pushing the door open, I head out to my car with a mission on my mind. Dr. Mark Franz has been asking me on a date for a while now. I've known him since I started working at the hospital. He got divorced a few years ago and about six months ago he asked me out. I've always felt like the boys needed me more than anyone else, but maybe it's time for me to go accept that date invitation.

As I drive out of the parking lot, I glance back in my rearview mirror and allow myself one more moment to think about what might have been.

~*~

"I'm glad you finally took me up on my dinner invitation," Mark says before taking a sip of his wine.

I smile and nod. "I am, too. I know it took me a while, but I hope it was worth it."

He smiles. "I assure you it is."

"So you have two kids, right?" I ask before taking a bite of my salad.

"Yes, a boy that's six and a girl that's ten." He shows me a picture on his phone. "They're great kids."

"Have they done okay since your divorce?"

He nods. "Well, my youngest doesn't remember much, he was only three, my daughter, she took it a little harder, but she's adjusting. How about your son?"

"Well, my ex left the day I found out I was pregnant, so Loxley really has no memories of him. He's asked a few times, but with us having the twins all the time, too, I think it doesn't really bother him. I mean their mom and dad aren't around. So to him, having me and his grandparents is better than nothing," I say wiping my mouth and taking a sip of wine.

"I know you have your friend's kids all the time, I just didn't know how much." The look on his face tells me he wasn't aware I had so much baggage.

"Yeah, they pretty much live with me. I didn't plan on them, but I can't imagine my life without them now. I feel like they are as much mine as Loxley is." I know I'm coming off defensive.

He puts his hands up. "No, please don't think I'm saying that like it's a bad thing. I just didn't know."

I sigh, "Sorry, I get a little defensive of my boys. They're part of the reason I've taken so long to take you up on your offer. I don't want people floating in and out of their lives."

"Where are they tonight?" he asks.

I glance at my watch. "They should be getting to my parents' from the training."

"Training?" he questions.

"Yes, MMA training, or well the basics anyway." Vance agreed to drop them off at my parents' after they finished tonight. I still don't quite trust the three of them alone for a long amount of time. My house might not still be standing when I get back there.

His eyes show the shock. "You're letting them train to fight? In the MMA? How old are they?"

"They're thirteen, and it's not really the fighting part, it's more the discipline and training itself. The martial arts aspect of it," I answer, back on my defensive mode.

"How did they get into that?"

"Well, a few weeks ago they got into some trouble at school and ended up with a few *forced* days off. A friend of mine who just moved here was opening an MMA gym. He offered to put them to work helping him get it set up, do some light construction. It just worked out, they had to work during their time off, rather than sit on their butts at home and me lose days from work, and they learned some stuff. They kinda fell in love with the place and so I'm letting them do some training there," I explain, placing my napkin in my lap.

He looks concerned, for what I don't know. "Are you sure that's a good idea with boys their age, though? I mean, how well do you know this friend?"

I have to laugh, "I've known him most of my life. He's a former Marine, I dated him when I was younger and my dad thought it was an okay idea, too. Do I need to justify my parenting to you any more than that? Considering you've never actually met my kids?"

He raises his hands in defense. "I'm sorry, you're right. I've just never been a fan of violent sports. I think the same thing about hockey and football."

Oh shit, I hope he never says that in front of my father. The man who thinks they've made college football too much of a pussy sport with the penalties.

Move on, Elaine, you need to make conversation. Even if everything about tonight feels forced and off, I need to carry on. "Well, that's okay, not everyone likes sports."

"Oh, I like to play golf." Good lord, is that really considered a sport?

I clear my throat. "I like to read most of the time after the boys are in bed. What about you?" I ask, trying to move on from sports.

"Not much for pleasure, unfortunately. I mostly end up reading medical journals to stay on top of different surgical techniques," he replies.

We go back to quietly eating. I look around at the ambience of this restaurant. I mean this is a really nice place, there's twinkly lights, linen table cloths and linen napkins. They are bringing food out in courses. Seriously! I need to try harder. Have I really been out of the dating game so long that I can't make conversation?

"I'm sorry, I feel like I'm failing at this. I haven't been on a nice date like this in a long time. I'm used to wearing scrubs, getting puked on, talking to doctors in jargon and then going home to feed three bottomless pit boys," I blurt out.

"It's okay," he replies. "It was weird for me the first few times I went out after my divorce." Okay, so he's been on several dates since his divorce three years ago. Hell, I'm thirteen years out from my husband leaving and I'm a damn rookie.

"How long after your divorce before you went on your first date?" I ask.

"Well, we were separated for about six months and our divorce was in the process, but I wasn't technically divorced." Wow. Holy shit. I'm not bashing him or saying it's wrong, I don't know what the details of his marriage was, but it just is so foreign to me. "What about you?"

"Um, well, it took me until Lox was ten or so before my ex was actually found and signed the papers. I still don't know who really found him. I did go out on a date or two when he was around five or so. Just raising him by myself and the twins most of the time, working full-time to provide for them because I didn't want to rely on my parents, there wasn't a lot of time to date, I guess."

He looks up at me. "Wow, that's a long time. Not talking about the dating, which that's a long time, too, but finding him to get your divorce finalized. Did he pay you back child support?"

I shake my head. "No, I never asked for it. I just wanted to be rid of him. He wasn't a good person. He was a leach, he didn't work, he blamed me for everything and he cheated on me. The night I told him I was pregnant with Lox, I walked in and caught him with a bimbo on my couch. He was out of a job and told me to get rid of it, that he didn't need another mouth to feed."

He sits back a little bit. "Damn, he really was a piece of shit. I can see why you're so gun shy about dating." He leans up, resting his elbows on the table. "I'm sorry this has started off so stiff, let's just talk about anything. The hospital, the weather, whatever makes you comfortable. I want this to be a good experience."

"Thank you."

He holds up his glass. "Well, here's to moving on."

I smile and clink my glass against his. "I guess so. Thank you."

CHAPTER 18

MARCO

Sitting on the back patio of the Loxley house, the fall breeze starting to blow across, drinking a beer with Hugh, he looks over at me. "How are things going at the gym?"

"Good, picking up." I take a sip from the bottle. "The boys really helped me get some work done around there so I could get up and going."

"The boys doing good with the training?" he questions.

"Yeah, I'm just glad she's letting me work with them. I didn't think that was gonna be possible for a minute, she was not up for it. I think the only reason she gave in what little she has is because Huck talked to me. I mean actually talked to me." It still amazes me how much those kids have opened up to me.

He gives me a nod of acknowledgment. "So do you wanna tell me why my daughter is out on a date with some doctor tonight instead of you?"

I laugh, leave it to Hugh to be so damn forward about it. "Well, I'm not sure. I was not involved in the decision, but if I was a betting person, the doctor asked her out and I haven't."

"That's my point. Why haven't you? Instead you're here dropping the kids off." He shakes his head. "Not that I have a problem with you taking care of those kids in there because in my opinion it's great, just making a point."

"Look, she's just coming around to me and so are the boys. I know that my relationship with them is important to her. Knowing her, she's trying to separate church and state," I explain.

He nods. "Yeah, that's true. You know, she's only been out on a few dates since Lox was born. On the surface, I don't think she wanted to expose the boys to men, plus she really didn't have time. She's been working her ass off for years, but deep down I think it's because it wasn't you."

I shake my head, "I doubt that." Am I jealous as hell that she's out on a date right now? Yes, but if this is what she needs then that's what I have to accept. "But, if it's because of the boys, which is what I suspect, then I'm all for it. I'm finally making some ground with them." Even though it's only been a short time, I can't risk losing what I have with them. If something didn't work out, I'm afraid she'd take them away. What I'm doing with them means as much to me as it does to them.

He takes a sip of beer. "I'm glad the boys have you. That stroke slowed me down, finally made me retire. The wife and I enjoy traveling. Do yourself a favor and remember this, when you and my daughter decide to get your shit together and finally get married, don't let it take almost dying to get you to understand the importance of doing stuff with your family."

"Old man, you're acting like this is the end of your life and that it's a given that she's going to pick me eventually," I say with a laugh. "What makes you think I'm even worth that?"

He turns to me, tossing an empty bottle into the small trash can between us. "Son, if I didn't think you were worth it, I'd have killed your ass that morning in the motel room. But something told me then and it's still telling me now that you're worth every bit of it." Damn, he had to bring up that morning in the motel room.

I shake my head, "You know the day I walked up on that porch, the patrol car in the driveway, my long hair tied back, kid from the trailers, I thought for sure you were going to send me packing. Tell me to get the hell off of your porch and stay away from your daughter."

He gives me a deep laugh, "I thought about it. I really did, but the way you were so honest with me, had a plan, I saw a look of determination, a man in the making, so I let you in the house."

The back door swings open and Sly barrels out, "Pop, when is Mom supposed to be here? Those two are boring as hell."

"I don't know, whenever her date is over with, and watch your mouth," Hugh replies.

Sly flops down in one of the chairs. "Why is she on a stupid date anyway?"

"Because she wants to be, that's why. She's a grown woman," I tell him. "You know if we were at the gym right now you'd be giving me twenty-five for that language."

He nods, "Yes, sir."

I stand up, "I'm gonna head out. Hugh, thanks for the beer and the chat. Sly, go do some homework and you won't be bored."

"It's the weekend, I don't have any homework," Sly defends.

"Fine then, go read a book," I say, bopping him lightly on the head.

I walk through the house saying goodbye before heading out to my truck. As I open the door, Elaine pulls up in her car. I wait for her to get out. "Hey, are you just dropping the boys off?"

I shake my head. "Nah, I've been here for a little while. Had to have a talk out back with Hugh."

She laughs lightly, "Should I be jealous?"

"No, I think he just wanted to check in on things. See how things are coming along at the gym, how the boys are doing. That kind of stuff."

She shifts on her feet. "Things going okay with the boys?"

"Oh yeah, they're doing great. I can see a difference in them already."

She nods. "Good, I just really want to build up their confidence."

I smirk, "Sly wasn't too happy about you being on a date, though."

Her expression changes quickly, "What did he say?"

I shake my head and walk around to stand in front of her. "Nothing big, I think he was just bored and wanted to go home. There is nothing wrong with you going on a date."

"I don't want them to feel like I'm abandoning them or something." She leans back against her car.

I prop up next to her. "You are not abandoning them. Sly is just impatient and the other two must've told him to leave them alone. You didn't do anything wrong." I bump my shoulder against hers. "So how did the date go?"

She swallows. "It went okay. It was a little weird at first, but we ended up having a nice time and we plan to go out again sometime."

Damn, that felt like a kick to the gut. "Good." I glance at my watch. "Well, I've got a client coming in early in the morning, so I need to head out."

I walk to my open truck and climb in, waving at her. She waves back, "Goodnight, Vance."

"Goodnight, Lainey."

CHAPTER 19

ELAINE

Five Months Later...

Leaning against the nurses' station in the ER talking to my friend Tracy, she smiles at me. "So, big date tonight?"

"No, he's got a late surgery tonight and the boys have training," I answer, signing a chart.

"Has he met the boys yet?" she asks with a smile.

"No, we haven't met each other's kids. I'm not sure if we are *there* yet," I explain.

"Girl, y'all have been seeing each other for several months now."

"Yes and no, I mean with our schedules we've been out several times now, but it's not like it's serious enough for us to meet families yet," I try to explain, but I'm not even really fooling myself.

Kertin, another ER nurse, walks up with a smirk, "Well, if he really wanted to meet your kids he'd make some time. You certainly don't think you're the only nurse he's dating, right?"

"I'm honestly not worried about what you think, Kertin," I grumble, shuffling some papers on the desk.

A doctor comes running by, "We've got an incoming trauma!"

I take off jogging toward the ambulance bay as the ambulance pulls up. The paramedic jumps out of the back, "Female involved in a head-on collision, early thirties, pregnant, pretty far along from the looks of it, unconscious in the field. She came to for a minute or two in the ambulance, but went out again."

I look at her face and recognize her immediately, "Gloria!".

The ER doctor looks at me. "You know her?"

"Yes, her name is Gloria Beck, she used to work here, her husband is Dr. John Beck, the chiropractor."

"FHP found her ID in the car, I believe they are contacting her husband," the paramedic responds.

We rush her back into a trauma room. "She's in the last month of her pregnancy I'm pretty sure, I know we just had her shower a few weeks ago," I ramble out loud. The doctor looks at me sternly.

Tracy grabs my hand, "Elaine, why don't you let me handle this? Go wait for her husband, I'm sure it would be nice for him to see a friend when he comes in."

They start shouting out her vitals and I take Tracy's advice, going to wait for Beck to come in.

Kertin smirks a little when I get back to the desk. "What, couldn't handle your *friend* coming in?" I want to slap the hell out of her.

I sigh and place my hands on the counter. "Look, I don't know what your problem is and I really don't have the time to care. I am waiting on the patient's husband to come in. I can understand how you can't separate the two since you don't have any friends."

She practically snarls at me. "You're just jealous because I fucked Mark Franz before you."

My eyes pop open. "Excuse me?"

Just about that time, Mark steps up. "Hello, ladies. Elaine, I was wondering if you'd like to grab coffee if you have time?"

I turn to him, "Did you sleep with her?"

I point to Kertin. He swallows hard. "Yes, but it was just after my separation and it was nothing to brag about."

She scoffs and walks away. My heart is pounding in my chest. "So right around the same time you asked me out to start with?" I shake my head. "Wow!"

"Elaine, I'm sorry, let's go get some coffee and I'll explain," he pleads.

I start shaking my head when I see Beck come running into the ER. "I don't have time for this bullshit." I put my hand up to Mark, "I have to take care of something."

He tries to call out to me, but I walk straight over to Beck. "Beck." I throw my arms around him. "She's back there now, they're checking her out. They said she was in and out on the way here."

"What happened?" he pleads, his body physically shaking from the adrenaline.

"I'm not sure of the details, one of the FHP officers is still back there." I put my hand on his shoulder, "Come on, we'll go back there."

I lead him back to the area where we have family members wait while they assess someone. "They'll come out and let you know something as soon as they can. Do you want me to do anything? Call someone? Get you something?"

He shakes his head, sitting down. "I-I don't know."

"How about I call Vance?" He looks up at me, his eyes wrecked with worry and pain, and gives me a slight nod.

I step just outside of the room to the desk and call Vance. "Hello?"

"Hey, it's Elaine. I need you to get down here to the hospital. Gloria was in an accident, it's not good. Beck is here, but he needs you," I blurt that out as quickly as possible to keep me from bursting into tears.

"Okay, I'm on my way. Let him know." I hear doors slamming and noise in the background.

I let out a huge sigh when he hangs up. "Elaine, can we talk?"

I look at Franz, "No, now isn't a good time. A good friend of mine was just brought in; she's expecting a baby in the next month. Her husband is sitting in that waiting room, dying a little inside. So no, we can't talk." My hands are on my hips and my chest is visibly rising and falling from my breathing. I shake my head and turn to walk away. He grabs my arm.

"It's about your friend." His face is all seriousness. The look I see when they give a patient's family the worst news they can imagine.

I stop in my tracks and feel a roaring in my ears. I'm expecting him to tell me she's gone. "They are rushing her into surgery. I'm going in to assist, she has some internal bleeding and the baby is in distress. Right now, I want you to go sit with her husband. I promise we're going to do everything we can. The other surgeon is going in to talk to him now."

I do as he asks. My heart is beating so hard I can hear it in my ears, so loud it's drowning out any other noise in the hall. Another nurse comes in and they move us to a surgical waiting room. FHP has been in here and filled him in on the accident. Listening to the trooper recount the accident tears me apart. She was just minding her own business, probably on her way to the grocery store before going home, and this happened. Just normal stuff and someone came into her lane and hit her head on. We were told the other driver died at the scene. I feel so heartbroken for Beck, I can see the loneliness in his face. Gloria's parents are out of the country and are trying to get back, so Beck, Vance and myself sit in the waiting room for hours until Mark finally walks through the door with the other surgeon. I hold my breath.

"Dr. Beck," the other surgeon speaks. "Your wife had some major internal bleeding, she lost a lot of blood. We were able to do the repairs and while it's still guarded, she should recover from the accident fine."

Beck nods and swallows hard, "And the baby?"

The doctor sighs and his face says it all. There's a deep sadness and anguish in his eyes, I turn my head because I know what he's going to say before he says it. "I'm sorry, we did everything we could, between him being early and all of the trauma, it was just too much." My hand flies to my mouth and I have what feels like a large ball in my throat, blocking the cry that wants to escape.

A sob comes from him and Vance takes him in his arms. I feel like I'm going to throw up, but I do my best to keep it swallowed and not fall apart myself. I'm a professional, death comes with this job. Taking a cleansing breath, I motion for the doctors to follow me out into the hall. "Thank you guys for doing what you could do. Mark, what do we need to do now? What's the next step?" He reaches over and wipes the tears that have escaped no matter how hard I fought from my face.

He explains to me the next steps for the baby's body. In all of the years I've worked here, somehow I've been fortunate enough to miss this happening. He lets me know that they will be moving Gloria in the next hour to an ICU room.

I step back in the room and see a man who was about to have it all falling apart after having it snatched away from him. Sometimes the world is so cruel.

Vance's eyes connect with mine and I see it, that same pain I saw years ago. I need to put some space between me and him because I can't do this to myself again. The boys need him, but I need to stay away from him. My heart could never handle this. Where we are at right now is a slippery slope.

Right now, I need to worry about Beck and Gloria. I can worry about men another time.

CHAPTER 20

MARCO

June 2005

"Huck, keep your head together in there!" I yell from outside of the ring. "Sly, watch that jab!"

I watch the two of them spar and wonder where the third of the trio is. I see Huck slipping again. "Huck, what is going on with you, son?"

"I think he's having girl problems. Well, or maybe it's boy problems," Sly blurts out right before Huck gives him a pretty hard tap to the face.

Now, they're both pissed off. "Stop! Get out and cool off and tell me where Loxley is."

Sly grins, "He's probably on the phone with Mary Beth again."

I shake my head, rolling my eyes. These boys are fifteen now and girls are coming out of the damn woodwork.

As I round the corner into one of the training rooms, Lox is sitting with his back to me on a weight bench with the damn phone pressed to his ear.

"Yeah, well, I think you look really sexy in that cheer uniform. I'd really like to get my hands up that skirt. Sounds good, meet you there tomorrow." He ends his call and stands up. When he turns around and sees me, I can tell he wonders just what in the hell I heard.

I cross my arms over my chest. "Why are you in here gabbing on the phone with Mary Beth when you should be running on the treadmill? You'd get winded opening a bag of chips right now, you need to be training. That's what you're here to do, son."

"I wasn't talking to Mary Beth, I was talking to Ally," he says with an attitude.

"What the hell, Loxley? How many damn girls are you talking to like you were talking to that one?" I say, pure growling.

He shrugs his shoulders.

"Son, you need to think about what you're doing."

He glares at me. "You're not my dad. I don't need your damn advice."

That feels like a sucker punch to the face. It hurts. I know he's not mine, but that doesn't mean I don't think of him that way. "I know I'm not your damn father! I'm your trainer, so get your ass in there on that treadmill, I'll come get you when I decide you're done." I spin and walk out of the room and go to my office, slamming the door.

I've got to call Lainey. I was fifteen and having sex. I know she wasn't, but I was. Hell, I may already be too late, but someone's got to talk to them. Picking up my phone, I hit her contact and listen to it ring. "Hello."

"Hey, Lainey, I need to talk to you about something and I don't want you to freak out, okay?" I try to say calmly.

"Are the boys okay? Is one of them hurt?" Yep, she's panicking.

"No, nothing like that." I take a deep breath. "Listen, I think I need to have a talk with the boys about sex."

"Do you think they're having sex?" she practically screams.

"I honestly don't know, babe." Whoops, slip of the tongue. "I just know when I was their age I was, and they are all the time on the phone with these girls. I just think it may be better coming from me. You know, man to man kinda conversation. Unless you want your dad or Mark to talk with them." I can't believe she's still dating that damn doctor, but I don't really think the boys have much to do with him. She keeps it pretty separate. I'm pretty sure for her it's a defense to keep from getting too close to someone and letting them hurt her or the boys.

"I've talked with them about sex, I mean I'm a freaking nurse for crying out loud!" Her voice goes up several octaves.

"It's going to be okay. I'm sure it's just weird for them to talk to their mom about it. Okay?" I say, trying to calm her.

"Yeah, just don't tell me when you do it. All right?"

Oh, it's about to happen as soon as I hang up this damn phone. I may be too late already. "Sure."

"You're probably right anyway about them not wanting to talk to their mom about it and Dad, well, he's just..." The sound of her voice just hurts me, she sounds tired and defeated.

"What's wrong with Hugh?" I say, worried that something has happened with his health again. I never shed a tear when my own parents died, but if something happened to hers it would break my heart.

"Mom said he's been having some episodes and she's taking him to the doctor." She sighs, "It just seems to be one thing after the other here lately." I can't handle her voice sounding so full of hurt. I rub my hand over my face in frustration.

"What do you mean?" I question again. What kind of episodes? I'm wondering now.

"Well, my car has been giving me issues, this stuff with dad and then I broke things off with Mark the other day." I almost want to cry out in joy and I probably would if she didn't sound like she was breaking apart. I hear the tremble when she speaks.

"Let's tackle things one at the time. What happened with Mark?" Like I really fucking care. But, if he hurt her, I'll fucking kick his ass.

"He wanted more and I just don't think I'm ready to give it. I know the boys are fifteen, but they don't seem to like him and that's a big deal to me. I mean we ended on good terms so it won't be too awkward around the hospital, but shit, you don't want to hear about all of this."

"Yes, I do. You're my best friend and I hope I'm yours."

"I just didn't feel right about what he wanted and I didn't feel right dragging him along anymore. The last time I moved at someone else's pace, I had a deadbeat husband. So, I just put a stop to it."

"Well, if you're happy then I'm happy. I only want that for you, Lainey. Now, what is the car doing?"

I listen to her try and describe a sound that it's making. Which is hilarious in its own right. "Will you be home when I drop the boys off in a little while?"

"Yes."

"I'll check it then. Listen, I gotta go check on them, but I'll talk to you soon."

"Thanks, Vance."

"Bye, Lainey."

I storm out into the area where all three boys are now on some type of equipment working out. "Get in my office."

I hear them walking behind me, asking who did something.

We go into my office and I shut the door. "First off, I remember what it was like to be your age, so I am going to keep it short and sweet. Don't be screwing around with a bunch of damn girls. If you do, for the love of everything, make sure you wrap it up."

Lox still stands over there with a chip on his shoulder. "How is what we do any of your business? Yeah, you're our trainer, but not our father. You're just some guy my mom used to screw in high school and has always been hung up on." Where in the hell did this kid's mouth come from?

I step right into his personal space and I see the other two take a step back. "Do not ever talk about your mother that way. I did screw around before your mom and it was stupid. Your mom changed me for the better and she didn't screw around. I'm trying to keep you from fucking up your life just because you've got a damn chip as big as Texas on shoulder and wanna get your dick wet."

He steps back a little and looks at the other two. I speak again. "Now, as I was saying, I may be too late for one, two, or hell all three of you," looking at their faces I know I'm right about everyone but Huck. "But if you are going to have sex, wrap it up. Every freaking time. Don't trust some girl just because you are desperate to feel a pussy on your little teenage cock."

Before they can respond about anything, I bark at them to go back out and workout. I write myself a note to hit up CVS and grab a box of condoms to let them know is here just in case. Sitting at my desk, I open my email and see one from Beck. He's saying that he and Gloria will be in St. Augustine and want Lainey and me to come see them.

That gives me a smile. He and Gloria left not long after the accident. They were both in a dark place, but his was so dark that I thought I was going to lose him. I called an old friend of ours that was a chaplain in the Corps, he came down and talked to them. Ultimately, he invited them on a mission trip. They went and ended up deciding to close the practice and work in different countries, helping out people who can't help themselves. It's been a good thing to help them heal. I reply to him that I will see him and I will let Lainey know. I forward his email to her letting her know that I plan to go. She almost immediately replies that she wants to go, too. I get up from my desk with a smile and walk back to see what the trio of trouble is doing.

~*~

A few hours later, I pull into her driveway with the boys in the truck. "Okay, I have to check on something with your mom's car. Why don't you guys stay out here and help me? You might learn something or you might not. I don't claim to be a mechanic, so this could be a crap shoot."

They all laugh as they lumber out of my truck. "Pop taught us some stuff," Huck replies. "So we might know something."

I nod my head at the door, "One of you go let her know we're here."

A minute or two later, she comes out with her keys. She once again tries to tell me what is going on which only results in the boys laughing.

I slide the seat back and get in the car to crank it. I rev the engine and cut it off. "When was the last time you got the oil changed? It's running rough. Sounds like a diesel truck."

Her face turns a little pink as she thinks. "Um, I'm not real sure. It might be a little overdue," she says, shrugging.

Huck looks at her. "Have you taken it anywhere since Pop and I changed it a few months ago?" Her face tells me everything.

I tip my head back. "Lainey, you seriously haven't changed your oil in…" I look at the little sticker her dad put in the window and then turn the key to see her odometer. My eyes bulge, "Nearly eight thousand miles?!"

"Mom!" Huck yells.

"Pop is going to have a freakin' fit." This comes from Lox.

Sly nods. "Yeah, he tells you all the time to keep your car serviced."

She glares at them. "I do not need the three of you trying to parent me."

I shake my head, "I'll call a friend of mine to come and get it. You can't drive it anymore. You'll risk making things worse."

She puts her hands on her hips, clearly frustrated. "How am I going to get to work? Not to mention going to see Gloria this weekend." She runs her hand over her head. "I guess I'll just have to stay home. I can borrow Mom's car to go to work tomorrow, but I can't take it out of town." By the time she finishes this rant I can see the exhaustion taking over, she's about to cry and one thing I can't handle is seeing Lainey cry. Clearly there has to be more going on.

I look over at the boys who are still laughing because they're teenagers, what more can I say? "Boys, go on inside and I'll help Lainey get the car ready to go." After they walk in the door, I walk closer to her. I can see the stress all over her face as I pull her into my chest. "Lainey, what all is going on? I know you told me a few things today on the phone, but there is something bigger here."

I hear a sob come from her. "It's just a lot right now. Dad, Mark, the car, the boys."

"Let's go sit over here on the porch for a minute. You tell me what's going on," I say as I pull her toward the swing.

She shakes her head. "Has Lox seemed off to you?"

I shrug, "Yeah, but I've amounted it to being a teenage dickhead boy."

"I was picking up a few things in his room the other day and bumped into some stuff on the dresser." Oh shit, she found something of a girl's or condoms or something like that. Nothing good can come from a teenage boy's room. "An envelope fell from his dresser." She shakes her head, "I don't know why but I opened it. It was addressed to him with no return address, but I still opened it."

My heart speeds up and I can see whatever was in that envelope is tearing her apart. "Lainey, you're scaring me."

"It was from Jeff." Her voice is broken and it comes out in almost a sob.

My emotions go from scared to angry in a heartbeat. "What in the hell did he want?"

"It was just like he was introducing himself and saying he was sorry he hadn't been there for him. That he loved him, but *I* didn't want him in his life. Just crazy stuff. Then I thought about how moody he's been lately and it just makes sense. I can't believe he hasn't told me about it." Her eyes show me all of the worry and pain she is carrying and I want to take it away.

"Well, he has been off the charts moody lately, but like I said before, I thought it was just a teenage thing. He hasn't said a word, though." I told that son of a bitch to stay away from them when he signed those damn papers. "Do you want me to talk to him, take the other two so you can talk to him alone, or sit with you while you talk to him? I'll do anything for you, Lainey."

She shakes her head. "No, I don't want him to think I'm snooping in his room and going through his stuff."

I rub her shoulder. "All right, here's what we're going to do. We'll leave the Lox thing alone for now. We'll go get your mom's car for you to drive to work, then you can ride with me to see Gloria this weekend and try to get rid of some of the tension you're carrying around." She looks up at me and I can tell she's about to launch some kind of argument. "You need a break, babe, you are juggling a lot right now. Please, don't make me pull your parents into this argument, because you know I will and you know I'll win."

She wipes her face and half laughs at me. "I swear, sometimes I think they love you more than me."

I shake my head. "Never. Now, let's get all of this stuff moving along."

She levels her eyes with mine and speaks softly, "Vance, thank you so much. I don't know what I'd do without you."

I watch her walk into the house and I shake my head. What did I just get myself into? Me and her riding together and spending the weekend together is just a recipe for our hearts to shred.

Before I leave town, though, I have some tracking to do. I'll find Jeffery Storm's ass one more time and figure out what he's up to.

CHAPTER 21

ELAINE

Why do I continue to do this to myself with a man I can't have? Riding in the same vehicle as Vance to see Gloria and Beck is a mistake. The two of us in close quarters like this never works well for us. He hurts me or I hurt him. I know deep down he was hurt when I finally did move along and get married. This time it would be the boys who got hurt if we got together and things didn't work out between us.

I need to break the tension in this car, the only safe topic I think we really have is the kids. "So, I know I asked you not to tell me, but did you talk with the boys?"

He clears his throat, "Um, yeah, I did."

Okay, clearly this is probably something that is going to give me nightmares. "I probably don't want to know, but how bad is it?"

He tips his head to the side like he's trying to decide what to say next. "Well, no one is pregnant or anything. Do

I think they're having sex or have had sex? Probably, maybe not all three, but I think two out of the three."

I look up at the roof of his truck in desperation, I don't even want to know which two, "Good lord, what am I going to do with them?" I shake my head, "Please tell me they are at least being responsible and not sleeping with everything that walks."

He clears his throat. "We, uh, talked about that. I gave them my advice on not being ready for a family. I also went to the store and got a big box of condoms and put them in the cabinet in the locker room. I hope that doesn't piss you off or make you think I've over stepped, but if they're going to do this, I'd rather them have them available to them." He laughs, "Now, I didn't make a big production of it. I just said, 'In case your asses think you're grown, but aren't grown enough to go buy them.'" He and I both laugh for a second before I get back inside my own head.

I take a deep breath, realizing I'm in over my head with three teenage boys and sex. "No, you didn't overstep. I'm glad they have you. Honestly, some days I feel like I'm failing terribly when it comes to them."

He looks at me like I've lost my mind. "Lainey, you are the best thing that's ever happened to those boys and you could never fail them at anything. They think you hung the sun and moon." He grabs my hand with his. "Never, ever doubt yourself with them."

I squeeze his hand back. "Thanks, there are seriously some days, though, that I feel like I'm in over my head."

"Then you call me. I'll listen, I'll do whatever. I'll smoke them at the gym with workouts, knock their heads together if I have to." He gives me a small chuckle before bringing my hand up and giving it a gentle kiss before letting it go and quickly placing his hand back on the wheel.

He clears his throat like he realizes that he kissed my hand. "So did you hear anymore from your ex? Has there been anything else? Loxley still hasn't said anything and his mood is a little better."

I sigh, "No, I feel like that is another place where I'm just waiting for the other shoe to drop. I thought for sure when they finally tracked him down to sign those papers I'd never hear from him again."

"You weren't supposed to," he blurts out.

Wait a minute. "What?"

He lets out a heavy sigh. "I'm the one who found him, I'm the one who got him to sign the papers. I also told him to stay the fuck away from both of you."

I don't know whether to be angry or relieved. "Why hasn't anyone ever told me this?"

He drums his fingers on the steering wheel. "I told your dad I'd take care of it. He'd just had his stroke, they were worried about him coming back and wreaking havoc on your life. So I did what I promised." He glances at me and then back to the road. "Please, don't be angry with us. You had so much on your plate and that was something I could take care of for you."

I stare out the windshield for a few minutes digesting all of this. "Where did you find him?"

"He was in South Florida. Sponging off of another unsuspecting woman," he answers calmly.

"Really? So was this woman there when you delivered the papers?" I ask, now very curious.

He gives a short laugh, "Yep, and she kicked his ass out when I was leaving."

I laugh hard for a minute. "I should be pissed at you for butting into my business along with my daddy, but considering you made his life a little miserable, I'll let the two of you slide."

"Lainey, just promise me if he comes around or Lox gets another letter, you'll let me know. I'll go find him and reiterate my point," he says in a no-nonsense sort of way.

I nod, "Yes, I will."

He reaches up to scratch his face and asks, "Um, so Hugh, what's going on with him?"

I rub my hand over my face, trying to regain some sense of composure before I scream, because my life is starting to feel like it's spinning out of control. One thing I swore to myself after Jeffery was that I would always be in control. "Mom says the doctor told them he's been overdoing it in the yard and stuff, but they also changed up some of the medications he's on and told him he needs to cut back on the red meat and vegetables with vitamin K. Like collards, turnips, dark green leafy stuff. It makes the blood thicker and they're trying to thin his blood."

He snorts. "Oh, I'm sure he loved that shit."

"Oh yeah, he told the doctor to just go ahead and let him die because a life without steak and greens was a life he didn't want to live. Which started a whole argument between him and Mom." I shake my head. "They weren't speaking to each other when they got home." I chuckle almost maniacally. "At what point in my life did I become their parent, too?"

He shrugs. "Well, look on the bright side, I was always the parent at my house." Now, I feel like an ass.

I sigh, "I'm sorry. I know this is all pissy bullshit, but seriously, I had to referee an argument the other day in front of the boys about how many times that week they'd had beef. I mean come on," I cry out to the ceiling of the car.

He laughs, "How about this, I'll plan to go by and get Hugh one day next week and he can come *help* me at the gym. I'll come up with something he can do to give your mom a little break."

I smile at him. "That actually sounds really good."

"The boys have that amateur match coming up, I'm sure he'd like to watch them spar," he says, almost like he's thinking out loud.

I'm still not happy about the boys doing any fighting, but I also know the bigger the deal I make, the bigger they will, too. Which Vance promises me that these are very regulated matches with head gear and everything. So, I just have to trust all of them. Vance has repeatedly promised me the boys are good and have talent. It's just I'm their mom and I worry.

When we pull up in front of the hotel on the beach in St. Augustine that Beck told us to go to, it's like something out of a movie. Valet service, bellmen, the whole nine yards. I'm guessing this would be his in-laws' doing. Beck doesn't strike me as the type to blow money like this.

When we get out, the bellman follows us in with our bags and motions to the desk, "This way, ma'am, sir."

A lady gives us a bright smile, eying Vance up and down. "Hi, how can I help you?"

Vance steps up to the counter. "Ah, the reservation is in the name of Dr. John Beck. We're meeting him and his wife here. I'm not sure if they made it here yet or not."

The lady clicks on some stuff on the computer. "Yes, Dr. Beck called earlier. One of their flights got delayed and they won't be in until the early hours of the morning. He said to go ahead and check you guys in. He has a suite, we ran into a problem, though, and I informed him. He requested our three-bedroom suite, but all we have available is a two-bedroom. He told me you guys could make it work, though."

Vance nods, "Yeah, we'll figure it out. Did he say what time their flight would be in?"

She shakes her head and looks at Vance with a dreamy smile. "No, sir, he just said in the morning." She hands a couple of card keys over to us. "Elevators are to the left. Your room number is on the envelope. The bellman will bring your things up soon. If you or your sister need anything before they get in, just call down here we'll be happy to help you." She gives a smirk.

He nods, taking the keys. "Thank you."

We both crack up as we walk away and I snort, "Really, your sister?! Could she be any more blatant?"

"Come on, she was just doing her job," he says with a laugh, "albeit a little over the top."

I make my voice sound really girly and breathy, *"If you need anything, just call down here and we'll take care of it for you."*

"I guess I could've groped you right in front of her to show her you're not my sister," he says, half laughing.

"Whatever," I reply as the elevator goes up.

"So, who is getting the couch?" he asks.

I roll my eyes. "You, of course."

"Just like that?"

I laugh, "If you make me, I'll tell my daddy."

He scans his card at the door, opening it and holding the door for me to go inside. "Well then, right this way, madam."

When we walk inside, I think we're both kind of awestruck. "Damn, this is a nice place," Vance says with a low whistle.

"This screams Gloria's parents."

He nods. "Yeah, I think they have like some sort of timeshare or reward system, something Beck said."

I nod and look around some more. "Well, I have to say this is the classiest place I've ever stayed."

"So what do you want to do for supper?" he asks.

I shrug. "I really don't know." I thought I would get a little bit of a break after we arrived. That Gloria and Beck would be here to break up the tension, but now I'm winging it with bats flying around in my damn stomach. We still have that buzz between us, I can feel it, but I have to ignore it.

He looks through some pamphlet things on the table. "Hey, let's go eat at this place and then maybe do like that ghost tour or something."

I look at him like he's crazy. "A ghost tour, really? What are we, in junior high?"

"No, one of the guys that comes into the gym told me about it. They do a lot of history stuff on the tour and only scare you a little bit. I figured you'd like that kind of stuff," he explains.

That really is kinda sweet. "That sounds cool. So let's try that place for supper and then hit a ghost tour."

After freshening up for a few minutes, we head out. We take a shuttle from the beach over to the restaurant called Harry's. It feels like it takes us forever to get in, while we wait we get a brochure about the tour and call to get our reservation for later tonight to make sure we have plenty of time to eat and not rush.

I would really like to bring the boys over here one weekend. Maybe we could do the daytime tour. Huck really likes this kind of thing. Honestly, sometimes I swear he's more like me than Lox.

We make small talk as we order. The Cajun menu looks delicious, I can't wait to try our food. I swear Vance ordered a little bit of everything. "I need to go to the restroom really quick."

He grins, "Still a tiny bladder."

I wave him off with my hand. "Shut it."

Making my way to the bathroom, I go in and finish my business. Washing my hands, I feel the hair on my arms stand up. I glance around but don't see anything, so I shake it off and go back to our table.

Our food arrives as I do and we dig in. I freaking love calamari. "This calamari is awesome," I say to Vance.

He laughs, "Okay, just how much do you love it?"

I chew on a bite and answer. "So much that if I was on death row, that would be what I'd ask for."

He laughs, taking a pull from his beer bottle. "I've missed getting to hang with you, Lainey."

"What? We hang out all the time," I laugh.

"Only with the boys. Never just the two of us," he says, tipping his beer bottle toward me.

I think back and I guess he's right. "Sorry, I never really thought about it. The boys are my life and have been for so long, I guess I don't know how to just be without them."

He throws some money down on the table with our check. Glaring at him, I roll my eyes. "I wanted to pay for mine."

He waves me off. "You can do breakfast in the morning." Then he loops his arm through mine. "Now, let's go on this ghost tour."

A couple of hours later, I'm shocked as hell and he's laughing his ass off. "It's not funny, you asshole. I was in a fucking haunted bathroom. I felt the damn hair stand up on my arms. That chick was probably in there and I didn't even know it!"

He snorts as we walk to the shuttle. "Well, at least she didn't slap you."

I shove him in the arm. "Shut up!"

He laughs at me all the way back to our hotel. "I'm not ready for bed. What about you?"

I shrug, "Not really."

He motions to the other side of the lobby. "You wanna check out their bar?"

I laugh. "Well, let's see. I've had a shitty couple of weeks, I've got three teenage boys and I'm worried about becoming a grandma before they are adults. But this one weekend they're with my parents and I don't have to worry. Hell yeah, I wanna check out the bar."

He shakes his head and motions me that way. "Let's go!"

Sitting in the bar for an hour or so, we see all kinds of people coming and going. Some businessmen with young arm candy, some older rich couples. It's crazy as we people watch and make up stories about the people. We used to do this all the time when we dated, it was cheap entertainment for two broke high school kids. "Okay, so banker guy over there is in the middle of a divorce from his wife of twenty years and this young girl is just with him for his money and the sports car he just bought as part of his midlife crisis. He'll probably marry the new chic that I'm gonna call Kimmi with an I and in two years she'll leave him for the tennis instructor or pool boy."

He laughs at my version, "So does he ever regret leaving his wife?"

"Yes, but then it's too late because she's already moved on to a wealthy doctor and she's not looking back," I reply before starting to crunch on a piece of ice.

He studies me for a few minutes. Then he gets a serious look on his face. "So now that you've had a couple of drinks, do you want to tell me what really happened with *Franz*?" He puts his hand up, "And do not try to feed me the same bullshit you fed me in the yard the other day."

I shrug, "I honestly don't know. Mark is a great guy, but it's just not there for me. I don't feel like I think I should about him and I don't think it's fair to either of us to keep it up." I sigh, "I just feel he'd be better off to find someone he can really move on with and I'm just not that person."

He makes a face. "So he wasn't screwing around with another nurse or person? Anything like that?"

I shake my head. "Nope. He deserves more than I can give him." I take a deep breath, "He asked me to move in with him."

His eyes pop wide open. "What?"

I nod. "Yeah, I'm like you remember I come with three teenagers who eat more than an entire village, and he really didn't care. I just couldn't do it, though, I couldn't see myself or the boys being with him for the rest of our lives."

He grabs my hand. "Lainey, you aren't meant to stay alone for the rest of your life you know."

I shake my head. "We just didn't have that spark, that chemistry."

He barks out a loud laugh. "It sounds like to me you're saying he is a disappointment in the sack. That's what it sounds like," he says, laughing.

I snort and sit my drink down. "I'm not talking about that with you. You of all people will never get me to talk about it." I can't tell him that no other man has ever compared to him and this isn't something I care to joke about. I really don't want to hear about the women he's been with since me.

"Why not?" He waggles his eyebrows, "Hit a little too close to home?" He winks, "It's okay, babe, I know no man can live up to me." I know he's joking, but *it is* too close to home.

I swallow deep and it feels like a ball in my throat. "I just don't want to talk about it with you, okay?" I motion to the door. "I think I'm ready to go to bed."

I throw a few bills down on the table to cover our drinks and start walking toward the door. I can hear him following me. When we get in the elevator, he looks at me. "Listen, Lainey, I didn't mean to upset you in there."

I shake my head. "Stop, just stop. Please."

He tilts my head up to him, with me still fighting a little. I can't do this. "Lainey, I'm sorry. I thought we were just shooting the shit, you know. I was just kidding."

"I really can't talk about this stuff with you," I choke out.

"Babe, you're my closest friend and I want to be able to talk about things with you," he tries to reason.

The elevator opens to our floor and I hightail it to our suite. Once we're inside, I realize we never made a plan for sleeping, we joked but never decided. "I'll pull out the couch and get settled."

"No, I'll take the couch. I would say let's just use both bedrooms but Beck and Gloria may be in earlier than we get up," he says, almost rambling.

I shake my head, "No, you're way too big to try and sleep on the couch." I've got to clear my head. I need space from him. "I'm going to go take my shower. I'll get the couch ready when I get out."

Before he can reply, I escape to the bathroom and scold myself the entire time I'm in the shower, trying to forget what I'm upset about. Shutting the shower off, I look around and realize I forgot my clothes in my suitcase in my hasty retreat. I grab the robe folded up in one of the shelves and slide it on.

Stepping out into the room, I find Vance in his boxers setting up the sofa. "I told you I'm sleeping there, not you. So you don't have to set it up for me."

"If you really think I'm going to let you sleep there I'm afraid you don't know me at all," he explains, looking up at me for the first time.

I pull the robe closed tighter. "I, uh, forgot my clothes when I went in." I start rummaging through my suitcase.

"Hey, you can stay like that if you want, it's no hardship to me," he says with a smirk.

I start for the couch and he tries to block me. "I told you I'm sleeping here."

I shake my head. "No, you're not." I try to move past him but he blocks me again. "I need to move the pillows around and then go get dressed. Please stop."

I'm standing almost chest to chest with him. He places both hands along my jawline so that I have to look up to him. "God, you're still so beautiful."

I shake my head, trying to get loose from him. "No, a lot has changed."

He pulls my face closer and puts his lips on mine. Before I realize what I'm doing, I'm kissing him back. His lips greedily graze down my neck to my exposed collar bone as his hands slide down my arms. My breathing is coming out in heavy pants and I can feel myself getting wet between my thighs. He pulls at the belt on my robe with one hand, making it come open. He pulls back, looking at my now exposed body. "Damn, you still drive me wild."

I start to argue but before I can his mouth goes around one of my nipples while his hands slide inside the robe, going around to my backside and cupping the cheeks. He lifts me up and spins me around to the open sofa bed, laying me down on my back. He leans down, running his nose over my wet pussy. "You still intoxicate me."

I cry out his name, "Vance!" when his mouth latches onto my clit. His tongue laps away and he starts to apply pressure with a finger or two. Before long I'm going over the edge, coming on his face. He crawls over me and grabs for his wallet that he laid on the table. Taking out a condom, he rolls it on, I don't even remember him taking off his boxers. "No one has been like you," I say in a moan.

I feel the head of his thick cock at my opening as he starts to enter me. Our bodies move together like a dance, completely in sync with each other like we've never been apart. Our kisses are passionate and needy as our bodies mold together. Soon, we're both crying out as we come.

He rolls over, pulling me on top of him and strokes my back. "Damn, that was better than I even remember."

I chuckle. "No kidding. I guess we've both learned a little since we were eighteen."

His mouth is on top of my head kissing it and I feel him shake his head. "Nope, it's just you. How it's supposed to be."

A reality hits me. He sounds like he wants more than one night. We can't do this, if we did and messed it up it would be really bad for everyone involved, and the boys would never forgive me. I hear him doze off but my mind won't stop, until I finally just pass out from exhaustion.

A phone rings, waking me up and I feel him move next to me. He reaches over and grabs the room phone. "Hello," he mumbles out.

"Okay, well we didn't order anything." He waits a beat.

"Oh, okay then."

He hangs up the phone. "Well, I guess Beck had scheduled room service for each morning and they couldn't get us to answer the door."

"Oh," I say with a little blush.

The knock at the door comes a minute or so later. He grabs the robe off of the floor he pulled off of me last night and slips it on before he opens the door. "You can just put it on the table over there," he tells the staff member.

I can't do this. Last night was—holy shit, it was glorious, but we can't go into this with just our hormones. I have to think of the kids first. I've been doing a great job of that until now. One night alone and he has me on my back, crying out to him like he's the savior.

He starts uncovering the breakfast. "Well, this looks great. Are you ready to eat?"

"Yeah," I say, finally finding my words. "Let me just get dressed." I pull the sheet from the bed and grab some clothes, going into the bedroom.

I hear his phone ring in the other room and hear him talking to someone. Once I come out, he smiles at me. "Breakfast is served, ma'am."

"Was that your phone ringing?" I ask.

He gives me a sad look. "Yeah, it was Beck. Bad news. Some weather front came through and they couldn't get out. It looks like they won't be here until like Monday. He said the room is paid for until tomorrow if we still want to stay."

"Um, I don't know. Won't it be weird here just the two of us?" I say nervously.

He takes my hand and pulls me close. "What's wrong? What are you worrying about?" I shake my head but he won't let me get away. "I know you, Lainey, you are in your own head right now. What's wrong?"

I sigh and take a seat. "We can't do this. Don't get me wrong, what we had last night was great and I've never—" I swallow. "It's just if we try this and it doesn't work out, the boys will be the ones that walk away hurt. Not us."

He shakes his head. "Babe, that won't happen."

I butter my toast and shake my head. "No, it's not—we just can't—the boys' happiness is too big of a risk." I sip the water he poured for us. "Maybe when the boys are adults or something. Right now, they need you more than I need you."

He looks at me before he replies, like he's in deep thought and a little hurt. "I guess you're right. We'll wait and see what happens when they're older."

I hate that I'm the one hurting him this time. I can see it all over his face, but he goes back to trying to finish his breakfast like the man he is.

"Thanks. I'm sorry. I just can't risk it for them." I feel tears welling up in my eyes because truth be told, if they weren't part of the equation I would jump into his arms and never get down. I do my best to swallow some of the breakfast laid out in front of us without choking on it.

We eat in silence and then he abruptly stands up. "We should probably get dressed and hit the road then."

"Yeah, I guess we should."

Please, tell me I didn't just make the biggest mistake of my life.

PART III

CHAPTER 22

MARCO

Pensacola- 2009

I glance at my watch one more time. Where in the hell are those boys? Fucking nineteen years old and can't tell damn time.

Stepping into the elevator, I punch the button for their floor while shaking my head. "They better not have gotten shitfaced drunk last night in some titty club," I say to myself as the doors open and I stomp down the hall. I pound on the door. I hear them all whisper on the other side, when Huck slowly opens the door. "What is taking so damn long in—?" I stop, taking in the sight before me. "What in the ever loving hell, Loxley?"

He shakes his head. "Sorry, Marco." Glaring at Sly, he growls. "Can you put a fucking towel over me, please?"

Sly shakes his head, throwing a towel over Lox. "Dude."

I stand at the foot of the bed, so pissed I can't hardly see straight. If this got to any of the local papers or Elaine found out, I hate to even think of the repercussions. "Huck," I say through gritted teeth, "go down the street to the hardware store or a Lowe's and buy a damn set of bolt cutters. Cut these fucking cuffs off his dumb ass. Sly, you're coming with me because your fight is first tonight." I point at the other two. "Don't fucking waste any damn time getting that shit cut off and get your asses to the damn arena. Don't tear one damn thing up or I will kick your fucking asses." I turn around, grabbing Sly's arm on the way out the door.

He tries to pull away on our way to the elevator. "Come on, Marco, we just found him. It wasn't like we knew, and don't you find it a little funny?"

I put my finger in his face. "No, I don't. If this got out, the gym has MY name on it, Elaine would be mortified and you guys would never be taken seriously as professionals! Any more questions?"

He shakes his head. "No, sir."

Good lord, let's just get through this damn fight and get back home.

~*~

A few days later, I'm sitting here alone in my office after I sent the boys home and my cell phone rings.

"Hello?"

I hear sobbing in the back ground. "Marco." It's Huck's panicked voice.

I stand up, quickly grabbing my keys because I know I'm about to leave no matter what. "It's Gran." His voice cracks.

"Where are you?"

"At her and Pop's house," he chokes out.

"I'm on my way now," I say as I lock the gym door behind me, sprinting to my truck.

The drive to the Loxley's house is a blur. I know we've been dealing with Hugh's health over the past few years, but something being wrong with Nellie is a bit of a shock. From the sounds in the background it's bad.

Getting to their street, I already see an ambulance with lights going sitting out in front of their house. I pull my truck up in the edge of the yard to stay out of the way and jump out. I'll let Hugh get my ass for driving on his grass later. Running up to the door, I dart inside. Taking in the scene, I see Hugh sitting stoic in his recliner, Huck holding Lainey while she's sobbing and the other two boys holding each other. I see all of these things, but I don't see the EMTs rushing around, which to me is a bad sign.

Walking over to Huck, I pull Lainey from him and take her in my arms, holding her tight to my chest. Huck wipes his face and I motion for him to meet me in the kitchen, but he shakes his head violently. I hear voices coming from in there. I pass Elaine back to him and walk quietly into the kitchen where I see them loading Nellie up on the gurney. I pull a guy from the sheriff's department over to the side. "Can you tell me what happened?"

He studies me, "And you are?"

"A close friend of the family. I've known them since I was a kid. Elaine and I dated years ago."

He nods his head knowingly. "Vance DeMarco, Hugh has always talked about you." He glances back to the kitchen and speaks softly. "Hugh said she'd been feeling sick for a day or so, but nothing too bad. She came in here to start supper and he heard her hit the floor. He called 911 and then Elaine." He shakes his head. "She was gone almost immediately, though. Elaine and the EMTs think it may have been a massive heart attack. Elaine did CPR until the EMTs got here, but it was too late. She's been a wreck since, one of the boys has been taking care of her."

One of the EMTs steps over to him and says something. He nods and turns back to me. "Clancy's Funeral Home is here to pick her up." He glances to the living room. "I really don't want them to have to see all of this."

I nod my head. "You can use that door over there," I say, pointing, "It goes out through the back patio and there is a walkway that goes around to the front of the house."

He nods, going out that way I'm sure to let the funeral home people know how to come in. I head back into the living room. I touch Hugh on his shoulder and it's like he realizes I'm there for the first time. "Hugh, Clancy's is here. I told them they could go through the patio. Did you want to go back in there?"

He shakes his head. "No, son, can you just take care of it? I don't want Elaine or the boys dealing with more than they already have."

The next few hours are a blur but all in the same they seem to creep by.

As the night wears on, people from the neighborhood, sheriff's department and hospital start bringing food by. Hugh has been pretty quiet, but able to talk to people. I got Elaine up and took her to her old room to lie down for a little bit. The boys have talked to people on and off all night, but I need to make a point to sit down with them. First, I need to go check on Lainey, though.

I walk quietly down the hallway to the room I can remember sneaking in and out of as a teen. I push open the door, it's dark but the light from the hall shines in and I see her lying on her side, eyes wide open. I push the door closed and walk over, taking a seat on the side of the bed. "Babe, you need to eat something. That old lady from the hospital brought that white chicken chili stuff you're always raving about."

She gives me a soft smile. "I'll try to go get something in a little bit. Did Daddy eat?"

I nod. "Yeah, some of the people from the department have stopped by and he's visited with them on the patio. One of the guys got him to eat some chicken and stuff."

She swallows. "The boys?"

"They're fine, they're nineteen. I know this is hard for them, but they've visited and helped arrange things out there. It's going okay. I'd really like for you to come out, though."

She shakes her head. "I can't. I can't face those people and let them look at me and know I failed."

This confuses me. "You failed?"

"I never saw this coming and I couldn't save her. I am a fucking nurse with almost twenty years' experience in the emergency room and I couldn't save my own mother or see that she was headed for a massive heart attack. I know that's what it was, I saw the signs as soon as I looked at her." She rattles all of this out, crying and sobbing.

I pull her up to me and hug her tight. "Babe, listen to me. Nothing could prepare you for this. Nothing. You did what you could, but the EMTs said she was gone before she hit the floor. You couldn't save her. She wouldn't want you to feel this way."

She pulls back a little and looks up at me. The light from the moon coming through the window makes her eyes twinkle. "I don't know what I would've done without you today. I don't deserve to have you in my life, Vance."

I kiss her head. "I think you got it wrong, Lainey. I don't know what I ever did in my life to deserve you, but whatever it was I'm damn glad I did."

~*~

The next few weeks fly by, the funeral for Nellie was very sad. Lainey has been a mess but she's getting better, sounding more like her old self. Hugh has been his normal self, powering through each day, not wanting anyone to see his suffering. The boys have really stepped up and have been taking turns staying with him, since they still live with Lainey it all works out. All three of them have had their moments for their breakdowns and I've done my best to help handle them. I think for them, though, having the outlet in the gym has helped.

The twins have taken this really hard. I mean their biological grandma passed away a few years ago and it never fazed them really. I'm pretty sure their mom could die tomorrow and they'd be just like I was when my parents died, but Elaine and her parents have been their constant for so long they don't know anything else.

Looking over the boys' schedules, I've pushed their fights out about another month. They wanted to continue as normal, but I don't think that would be a good idea. I'm afraid they would go in there trying to prove something to the world and get hurt. Elaine would kill me and she just couldn't take it right now. She worries enough, she's never been one to come to their fights on a regular basis. She just can't stand to watch it. She comes when they have a big match up, but they nor I push her to do more.

They're all three decent fighters. They still have a lot to learn, though. That's why I told all of them that in order to fight for my gym, they needed to take a few college classes and get jobs. This way they'll figure out how bad they want to train. The boys are smart, but they really have no interest in school, I know this, Elaine knows this, but they need to fight for it. Also, a buddy of mine runs the local UPS shipping hub and got them jobs sorting packages on the evening shift so they can train during the day. He's also good about working around their fights.

My phone rings with an unknown number, but the area code is from out of the country which tells me it must be Beck. "Hello?"

"Hey, man."

"Beck, how the hell are you? How's Gloria and the kids?" Beck and Gloria adopted two siblings on one of their mission trips a few years back. That was actually one of the things they wanted to tell us when we were supposed to meet them in St. Augustine, that they were starting the process. Their kids are now twelve and fourteen. The kids are a little older than you might think someone would generally adopt, but he said when they saw them they knew they were theirs. I get it, though, those boys I worry about so much, who came into my life at thirteen, they became mine.

"Good. I have some big news." They must be adopting again. They've talked about it.

"Yeah, what is it?"

"We've decided to come home. I'm going to open my practice back up. I think Gloria may home school the kids until next school year to make sure they're where they need to be for the standards, but yep, we're coming home."

"Wow, man! That's great! I'll be happy to have your ass back here. But, what made you decide this?"

I hear him sigh through the crackly phone. "Some close calls recently." He pauses. "The kids, they've seen enough of this through their life already. I don't want them to have to endure that fear anymore."

I nod like he can see me or something. "I get it, man. You keep me posted about your plans and I'll do whatever you need me to."

"Good deal, thanks, buddy. Look, I need to go, but I'll be seeing you soon."

"See you soon," I say before I end the call.

I immediately send Lainey a text with the good news that our friends are moving home.

At the same time memories hit me of the night we spent together in St. Augustine. It was everything it needed to be, the way her body still responded to mine. How we still knew each other after too many years. Elaine freaked out, though, because of her just breaking up with Franz, and the boys. She said it couldn't happen again, that if anything we needed to wait.

I'm tired of waiting, though. The boys are adults now and I'm going to get my girl. Her mom dying so suddenly taught me we can be gone in an instant. I want her and even if we have to keep it quiet for a little while to keep from freaking the boys out, I'm fine with that. But she has to know how I feel.

> **ME: Meet me at the diner in an hour. I need to talk to you about something.**

> **LAINEY: Okay? I hope you aren't telling me I'm going to be a grandma or something. The way you've worded it my mind is racing on WTH the boys have done now.**

> **ME: Nope. Just need to talk.**

> **LAINEY: Okay...**

An hour later, I'm sitting in the diner when she walks in, worry etched on her face. She walks quickly over to me, I stand up and pull her into my arms and kiss her. My mouth covers hers and I take command, forcing my tongue between her lips to dance with hers. It's like there isn't anyone else in this room but us. This kiss is the kiss I've been missing since that weekend in St. Augustine.

She pulls away and looks at me confused. "Lainey, I love you and I'm tired of not being with you. The boys are adults. I understand if we want to keep this to ourselves for a little bit, but I need you and you need me." I motion between us. "This thing, this dance we've been doing for too many years. It's over now." I can feel her body trembling, like it does when she gets nervous. It takes me back to the first time we made love. "We'll be going out on dates and seeing each other as much as time allows. I don't want to drop dead one day and regret not having you in my life the way I want you." I reach up and brush her hair behind her ears.

She looks up at me with glassy eyes and swallows hard, nodding her head. "Okay. I'm yours."

You're damn right you are.

CHAPTER 23

ELAINE

November- 2015

Having the boys over for dinner makes me not miss them quite as much. "So Vance says you guys are possibly making plans to expand the gym and teach some classes?" I ask, more to make conversation than anything else. Vance and I have talked extensively about it. The boys still don't know we've been dating. It's crazy, but in all honesty, if they paid attention to more than the little floozies they run around with they'd see it.

"Yeah, sounds pretty awesome, doesn't it?" Sly says while he's taking a roll from the basket.

I nod. "Yes, it does. I think you guys would be wonderful at it." That's the reason I suggested it to Vance, but they need to think it's all part of the boys' club thing.

"We've already talked to a couple of girls about helping us train," Lox replies.

I sigh, "You guys better take this seriously. This isn't something to invite little tramps to and try to wrestle with them."

Sly snorts at my warning. Lox shakes his head along with Huck. "No, ma'am. These two girls I met through Dr. Beck. They're nice girls."

"And Lox has the hots for the massage therapist," Sly throws in.

"Wait a minute. When did you go see Beck?" I ask. Vance didn't mention anything about that.

"Marco sent me to him the other day after my last fight. My shoulder was giving me trouble, but it's doing better now. Doc said I probably just needed some massage therapy. Sloan hooked me up," he explains.

Huck glares at him while Sly snickers. "Dude, when we ran into her and that sexy chick Kara last night, you almost started drooling."

He glares at Sly. "I already told you she has no time for people like us."

Wait just a damn minute. Does this girl think she's too good for my son? "Hold up, what do you mean?"

Lox shakes his head. "No, I don't mean it like it sounded. She's a single mom, has a little five-year-old boy. Dad's not in the picture. She doesn't need some part-time fighter in her life messing it up. She needs someone stable." He shrugs, "I'm sure you get it, Mom, I mean that was you. Hell, it still is."

Damn, is this what I did? My kid thinks he's not good enough for someone because of how long I put off

Vance, or any man for that matter. Hell, I dated people I barely let him be around. That word "stable" sticks in my head. "Don't think like that about yourself." I rest my elbows on the table. "Sweetheart, I don't want you to think like that. As a matter of fact, you'll probably be one of the best to date her because you know how hard I worked. You'll understand."

Huck looks at me hard. He has something to say, I know it, but he's holding it until we're in private. He's always been like that.

The boys finish up with their plates and start cleaning up. I raised them to help out and do chores, so they know the rules. I cook, they clean up. While they're doing that, I step into the laundry room and start moving a load of laundry from the washing machine to the dryer and Huck follows me in. I turn around to face him. "Sweetie, is there something you want to talk to me about? You've been eyeballing me since dinner started and I can tell when something is going on with you."

He crosses his arms over his chest and leans back against the door facing. "Well, is there anything you wanna share with me?"

"What are you talking about, sweetie? You're staring at me like I used to look at y'all when you guys were younger," I say with my hand on my hip.

"Let's just say the other night I went by Marco's to drop off some papers, only when I got there your car was in the driveway." He shrugs, "Not a big deal, just thought you were visiting your *friend*. Only that isn't what I saw when I walked up on the porch and looked through the door."

He's visibly pissed. Huck has a big thing about keeping secrets. It's a trust thing for him. "Sweetheart—"

He cuts me off. "How long?"

Well, Elaine, explain it. "Since not long after Gran died. We wanted to keep things private because of you boys and your relationship with Vance."

"So, for what, like five years you've kept this a secret?" The vein is throbbing in his temple.

To be honest, though, I'm getting pissed. I don't have to explain myself to him. "Look, maybe we should've told you boys sooner, but here's the thing, it's our business. It's not like we've kept it super-secret, you guys could've figured it out by now, but you're so wrapped up in chasing tail you haven't seen it." Now he looks hurt. God, I can't win at this. "Listen, sweetie, I'm sorry. It's just we didn't plan for it to stay a secret this long. To start with our emotions were high because of Gran and then about the time that leveled out we lost Pop and there we were all over again."

"It's not that I don't like you being with him. I always wondered why you weren't, but I don't like feeling like I'm being lied to," he says, less gruff than before.

I pull him to me and hug his chest since he's so much taller than me. "I love you, Huckleberry. I promise we're going to talk to everyone soon. We were just talking about it the other night."

He nods and swallows hard. "Okay, I'll wait for you guys to say something."

I pat his cheek like I did when he was little. "Thanks, now tell me about this girl, Sloan. Is she good for Lox?"

He gives me a smirk. "Oh yeah."

~*~

Later in bed, I talk to Vance on the phone. "I think we should tell the other two this weekend after their fights," he says.

"Yeah, Huck will only hold off so long. I hate that it feels like such a betrayal to him," I say softly.

"Babe, it's not a betrayal. He's just a little hurt we kept it from him and the other two. Just goes to show you that we don't always know what in the hell we're doing."

Something pops in my head. "Oh yeah, I have a bone to pick with you in the interest of keeping secrets."

"Okay?"

"So my child had to go see Beck and I wasn't told. Go ahead and explain that to me."

He clears his throat. "How did that come up?"

"Well, they were telling me about this Sloan girl that Lox met and it came up. However, that doesn't matter."

He sighs. "Lainey, it wasn't a big deal, he just strained something. If it had been serious I would've called you. You know that."

"Yeah, I do. Sorry, you know how I am about the boys," I say, trying to calm myself a little bit.

"You should come to the fights more often and you'd see how good they are and how little they actually get hurt," he says with a little lilt of laughter in his voice.

"You know I can't do that. I can't watch my babies fight." I glance at the clock on my nightstand. "I need to go to sleep. I have a lot of reports to finish in the morning when I get in to work."

"Okay, babe, I love you and I promise we can talk to the boys soon. In the meantime, I'll chat with Huck and smooth things over."

"I love you, too."

I roll over and tuck my pillow into my side. *Why haven't we told the boys before now? It sounds stupid to say, but I really think time has just flown by us. We can't keep letting time fly by, it goes much faster than we think.*

CHAPTER 24

MARCO

Sitting in my office with Huck under the guise to discuss his weight class change, he stares at me. "Lainey called me."

His eye brows lift like he's studying me. "So, what do you have to say about it? I've heard her version."

I drum my hands on my desk, this kid thinks he's going to talk to me like a parent. "First off, we don't need to explain anything to you. You know I love you like you're mine, but you won't come in here like you're grown. You might be twenty-five, but in my eyes you're still that pissy kid I saw in the grocery store at ten years old giving me the evil eye." I clear my throat. "She has always been nervous about our relationship being more after the three of you came into the picture. She never wanted it to hurt the relationship that I have with y'all. Like she said, time has just gotten away from us." I chuckle, "Honestly, though, you boys have to be partially blind. We're always together. When we go out of town, you boys share a room and we share a room." I wave my hands around. "Do you see where I'm going with this?"

He rubs his face, "We just thought you guys were best friends and shared a room to save money. Did Pop know about this?"

I laugh, "Who do you think pushed us back together so hard after your Gran died?"

He leans back in his chair and stares at the ceiling. "You have to tell the other two soon or I will."

"We will—" We're interrupted by a knock on the door.

"Yo. Marco. There is someone here to see you," Lox's voice calls from outside the door.

Huck walks to the door and swings it open wide, eyeing the girl on the other side up and down. "Whatever she's trying to sell, I wanna buy some."

Lox shoves him and I pop him in the back of the head. "How can I help you, sweetie?"

Huck steps past her as she steps in, fidgeting nervously. She looks familiar in a way I can't place. She's a pretty girl, though. She glances up at me and it's like I get hit in the chest. "Um, well, I was told that you're my father."

I stumble back into my desk. Huck's eyes look like they belong in the cartoon he was named after. Lox steps back in the door. "Marco, you okay?"

I give them a quick nod, but my brain is going a million miles per hour. "Yeah, um, can you give us a minute?" I know what she's going to tell me, she looks too much like her mother to tell me anything any different.

He nods and pulls the door shut as they walk out.

I clear my throat, "Can you just give me a minute?"

She nods. "Yes, I'm sure this is a shock to you. If it helps it was to me, too."

I sit down and rub my face. "You look so much like Rosalinda, she never... How—?" I can't even finish my sentences.

She takes a seat across from me. "Let's start over for a second with my name. I'm Elizabeth Haas, my mother was Rosalinda. She passed away not too long ago and before she did, she and my dad, well, Haas were arguing and he yelled something about always knowing I wasn't his. I asked her later. She told me about you. She was really sick so I couldn't leave her and then it took me some time to find you after she died. I needed to get away from him after Mom died. He's always hated me, for several things, but now I know why it started."

I shake my head. "I'm so sorry. If I had known, I would've—" What would I have done? I have no clue. There are very few times in my life where I've ever felt this gutted. I have a kid, a beautiful kid, that was kept from me.

She puts up her hand. "I know, my mom explained your relationship to me and what happened during the last few days she was alive. She made me promise to never blame you. That you were one of the greatest people she'd ever known and that she regretted staying with him every day since."

I feel the tear roll down my face and I wipe it quickly. "Your mom was a great person, too, just stuck in a bad spot. He had a lot of power over both of us."

"I know you believe me, and I don't want anything from you other than to get to know you. I would like to get a DNA test, though, just to satisfy myself more than anything."

I shake my head. "It's really not necessary. I believe you."

She nods. "I know, but I need to see it in writing. My whole life, I felt out of place with him and now I find out that I was right all along and she kept it from me. I just need to see the evidence that it's all true."

This poor girl has been through the ringer I can tell, she's mentally beat down. "Whatever you need."

"So, um, are those guys—?"

"My sons?" I shake my head as she nods. "Not biologically. It's a long story that I'd like to tell you sometime, but I think for today we've touched enough. Would you be interested in coming to dinner at my house tomorrow night?"

She nods. "Yes." Then glances at her watch. "I really need to get going, I have a job interview."

"Do you need some help getting settled here?"

She shakes her head. "No, I'm fine."

I stand up. "Okay, let's go introduce you to the trio, I'm sure they're gossiping like little old ladies in the beauty shop out there."

She laughs and follows me out. I need to call Lainey, I need her there tomorrow night. This may put a small kink in our plans to tell the boys.

After filling the boys in, I go back to my office and get ready to leave for the day. Huck steps in my office. "You okay?"

I nod. "Yeah, I just need to get going and clear my head. Look, I'm going to talk to Lainey about this now and Elizabeth is coming over to my house tomorrow night for dinner, I just—"

He puts his hand up. "I get it, you need a little more time. It's okay. This is a big deal, Marco, but we've got your back."

I nod as I go out of my office and down the hall to the front doors. After getting in my truck, I call Lainey, and she answers quickly. "Hey."

"Are you at your house?"

"Yeah?" I can tell she's worried now.

"I need to talk to you, in person."

"Just come on over. Are the boys okay?"

I smile. "Yes, the boys are okay. I'll be there in a minute."

Once I pull up in front of her little ranch-style house, my breath feels like it releases after the whole drive here. She meets me at the door, concern all over her face. "Baby, what is going on? You're scaring me."

I drop onto her couch and rest my elbows on my knees. "I-I have a daughter."

She sits beside me. "What?"

Over the years I've told her about Rosalinda and other things from my Marine Corps time. "Rosalinda, we had a daughter. She never told me."

"H-Wh-Oh my god. How did you find this out?"

I clear my throat, trying not to choke up. "My daughter came to see me today. Rosalinda recently passed away and she told her then. Elizabeth is her name and she came to find me."

"Wow. Just. Wow." She pulls me into her arms and hugs me tight. "What do you need me to do?"

"I invited her to my house for dinner tomorrow night. I'd like for you to be there. I told her I would explain my relationship with the boys and anything else she wants to know."

"Do the boys know?"

"Yeah, they were there for it all," I say with a chuckle.

"Were they okay?"

I nod, "You know Huck got a little defensive, but we cleared it up. I really didn't talk to them much, I was in shock."

She rubs my short hair. "Yeah, I bet. Well, I'm here for you." She sighs, "And that poor girl. She's probably confused and just lost her mother. Bless her heart."

I take her face in my hands and kiss her hard. "You're the best thing that's ever happened to me."

"Same here," she whispers back.

Grabbing her waist, I pull her onto my lap and she straddles me. "God, I need you."

I push her scrub top up her arms and over her head, kissing down her neck to her collar bone and then down to the tops of her breasts. "You're perfect."

I stand up, wrapping her legs around my waist and carry her down the hallway to her bedroom. Laying her down on the bed, I quickly pull the string on her pants and tug them down her legs.

I lean down and kiss a trail up the inside of her thigh to the satin panties that cover her wet pussy. I grab the waist and tug them down to the floor with her pants and place my face right back into the wet heaven that awaits me.

Her body rolls and writhes under me. Reaching for my arms, she pulls me up her body and tugs my shirt up to take it off. I unclasp her bra and pull it off as she pushes at my gym shorts and underwear. Crawling on top of her, I sink right into her. "God, this is heaven," I groan out. Over the years, our sex life has grown to complete comfort. Not comfort as in boring, but comfort as in knowing what each of us like and thrive for.

Today we didn't fuck, today we made love. She knew what I needed and just how I needed it. She met me for every kiss, every thrust, every moan and every touch.

After we finish, I lie there watching the ceiling fan go around and around. Thinking how much I've missed in my own child's life. I've been there for the boys for all of these years and wasn't there for my own child. Worry eats at me all night and nerves eat me up the next day.

~*~

The day feels like it's dragging until it's time for dinner. Lainey is making her lasagna for us tonight and she keeps telling me not to worry, but I really feel like such a jackass. I've had a kid for all of these years and I never knew about her. I want to be pissed at Rosalinda, but I can't. What we had was at the wrong place and the wrong time. She was a great woman, she was in a no win situation, but she wasn't the woman I was meant to spend my life with.

"Vance, baby, please sit down here at the counter and drink a beer while you're waiting. You're making me nervous with all of the pacing you're doing. She's already told you that she doesn't blame you, that her mother didn't blame you. So let yourself off the hook." She smiles at me, "Please, for me."

I do as she asks and sit down with the beer she got out for me. Trying to relax, we make small talk about the boys' upcoming matches, and the girl Lox is sniffing around, Sloan. How I think Sly has a thing for Sloan's friend. I'm in the middle of telling her about the young guy I have named Gibbs when the doorbell rings.

I let out a big breath and make my way to the door. Opening the door, Elizabeth is standing there. She looks so much like her mother, but I can see small parts of me. "Hey, uh, come on in," I say nervously, stepping back from the door.

"Hey," she replies as she comes in.

Elaine comes in the foyer about that time. "Hello, you must be Elizabeth." She puts her hands on Elizabeth's shoulders. "You are such a beautiful girl." Elaine shakes her head for a second. "I'm sorry, I'm over here fawning all over you. I'm Elaine, Vance and I have been friends for years, since we were in high school. I think you met my terrible trio at the gym the other day."

Elizabeth gives a little laugh. "It's okay. It's nice to meet you, Elaine, everyone calls me Liz and yes, I guess I did meet your sons the other day." She motions between us. "So are you guys—?"

Elaine saves the day when she puts her arm around Elizabeth's shoulder, "Honey, that is a long story. I'm about to pull the lasagna out of the oven. Come with me and I'll do my best to explain."

I shake my head as I follow the two of them and listen as Lainey does what she always does. Makes everything better.

~*~

As the months go by, so many new people have been brought into our little functioning dysfunctional family. Liz and I have formed a pretty close relationship. She and Huck still have this tension between them, though. I don't understand it but I know with him it takes him some time to warm up to people and trust them.

Lox recently proposed to Sloan, she's great and her kid Sage (well, Slick, as Huck named him) comes in all the time. He's my Mt. Dew and Reese's Cups buddy.

Her friend Kara ended up in a mess with a kid I kicked out of here years ago named Drake. She and Sly have a baby together now, deep down I know the baby isn't Sly's and he knows it, too, but he'll never say a word. Sometimes I wish I'd have done that with Loxley. Krista is a beautiful, sweet little girl and she has all of us wrapped around her finger. She gave us all a scare getting here, but once she got here, she's perfect.

Speaking of our princess, glancing at the clock on my desk, she should be here soon with her daddy and uncle. Huck has a lot on his mind. He shared with me the other day that a couple of kids, a boy and a girl, came to him claiming to be his twin half-siblings. The stories match up, but Huck wants to be positive before he tells anyone else. He says the kids, Gia and Eli, seem like great kids, just a little lost.

Loud voices down the hallway break me away from my thoughts and then I see Huck run by with keys in his hand so I go to see what is going on. In the break room slash nursery, I find Sly sitting on the couch holding Krista close to his chest and Lox watching something intently on the TV while talking quietly to Sly. "What's going on, boys?"

Lox looks up. "Detective Harmon was killed today in the line of duty." Detective Harmon helped save Kara and Krista when her ex, Drake, tried to kill her.

I sink down in the chair. "Damn. He was a good man. I didn't know him all that well before this last incident with Drake, but he's a good, strong man." I drop my hands against the chair. "His wife is battling cancer, too."

The boys both shake their head and I clear my throat because this hits me probably harder than it should. "Just goes to show you can't take one day for granted." I let out a deep breath. "Lox, we need to talk."

I can see the worry etched across both of their faces, before I speak. "Lox, your mother and I have been keeping company for a few years now."

Sly chokes a little on his own spit and Lox's eyes look like a cartoon character. "Keeping company how, exactly?" Lox says slowly, then he shudders. "Never mind, don't tell me."

"Lox. Look at me, son. We went on a date right after you boys graduated. We've been seeing each other causally since. She's never wanted to make much of it because she was afraid that if it didn't work out between us, you boys would have to choose. Well, now that we're bringing daughter-in-laws and grandbabies into the fold, we're going to be in each other's lives forever. I want to marry your momma, Lox."

"Holy shit," Sly blurts out.

Lox looks at me harshly, a face I haven't seen since he was a fifteen-year-old teenager. "You really love her? This isn't some midlife crisis or something?"

I laugh, "I'm a little past midlife, but thanks. No, I love your momma, days like we've had the past couple of months make me see we can't keep putting off life. So, I'm going to ask your permission to marry her. The same way you asked Slick's."

Lox bolts up out of his chair and I stand to match him. Lox pulls me into a big hug. "You have it, old man, but I'm not calling your wrinkled ass daddy."

Sly raises his hand. "I will."

I point at him. "I'll beat your ass."

Walking out of the room, I call Lainey. "Hey, sweetheart," she says.

"Hey, I know you guys probably have a mess going on right now, but I just wanted to tell you I love you and I told the boys, well, Sly and Lox, that we're getting married," I blurt out. This is one of the moments in my life I've waited way too long for.

She laughs, "Well, how did they take it?"

I laugh, "Well, apparently those two pay attention to nothing because they were completely shocked. Hell, since Huck caught us, I thought we'd been pretty open over the past few months."

"Well, honey, they've both had a lot going on to distract them. How is Sly doing? Sloan called me about Kara."

My seriousness comes back. "He's pretty shook up, I think he'll feel better once Sloan brings Kara here. I know you've been crazy with all of this at the hospital. I don't know where Huck went but he ran out of here like his ass was on fire."

"He just came in here. He was looking for Detective Harmon's daughter. She works here. I just put it together in my head that she used to tutor him in high school. He looked very upset, he was heading to their house."

"Oh, okay. Well, I'll let you go, babe. I love you."

"I love you, too," she replies sweetly before hanging up.

Even with so much chaos, I'm happy my life is finally going where I need it to.

CHAPTER 25

ELAINE

I watch as Vance, Loxley, Sly, Huck, and a few others pull out in a rented van to drive to North Carolina for a friend of Vance's funeral. I only met Roundman briefly when he and some of his guys came through town and helped the boys with something, but he was kind. I could tell he thought the world of his beautiful daughter. My daddy probably would've had a fit knowing that Vance had asked for some help from a motorcycle club, but I also think he could've realized that with the situation we were in, the boys weren't sure who could be trusted. The Hellions MC members that I met seemed like good people.

Walking back inside the house, I smile at the wall of pictures in our foyer. I look at the picture I have from when the boys were about six or seven. It was Lox's birthday and they all have little party hats on and cake all over their faces. God knew I would need the twins, too, that's why he put them in my life. Lox would've been an only child. I hate that their mother became the trash she was, but I'm grateful I was there for them. Those three boys needed each other. If they hadn't found each other I'm afraid of who they'd be now. Lox would probably be some lonely guy; he would've never made the move to talk to Sloan. Sly would've probably used up all of his nine lives being ridiculous. Huck, my sweet broody Huck, I'm afraid he'd be in jail for the temper he had. The temper that Vance helped harness and turn into something productive.

I run my hand over the family picture from the gym last Christmas that makes me laugh, my three boys, Liz, Gibbs, Sloan's brother Jacob, Sergio and the twins' brother Eli. Along with all of their wives, girlfriends and kids, Vance and I are sitting in the middle of all that chaos.

Taking the picture to my chair, I sit down and study the people in it. So many people have come into our lives over these past few years. People I now can't imagine living without.

Sitting the picture down, I pick up some brochures for the vacation Vance and I have coming up. He's taking me to Greece for our anniversary. He says we've wasted enough time not being together, he wants to spend every moment we can together. The boys are running the gym pretty much, but Vance can't stay away. He still likes to help them prep for fights. Huck runs the business side of things along with the help of Paige, another person who was brought into our lives for a reason. I'm so proud of my boys, though, they work so hard and you'll never find more devoted husbands and dads.

I was talking with Lox one day after Linc was born, about how well he was doing being a dad, and how sorry I was for what had happened with his dad. How he was never around. He made my heart burst wide open when he said, "You were enough for both parents, Mom, but when you decided to let someone in our lives you gave us Marco, and he's shown me the kind of man I can be."

A knock on the door makes me set the stuff down. Opening the door, I find my three daughter-in-laws complete with grandkids. Bless Chelsea's heart, she's miserably pregnant with the newest addition. Sage, being the little helper he is, is holding his little brother Linc and Sly and Kara's daughter Krista's hand. Sloan has her hands full of groceries, while Kara has new baby Selah and Chelsea is holding little Harm's hand. I smile, "Well, this is a surprise! To what do I owe the pleasure?"

Sage hugs me tight, "Hey, Grandma." I kiss the top of his head and Krista and Linc hug my legs.

Sloan groans from behind the bags. "You have double ovens and Kara's lovely husband signed all of us up the other day for some bake sale thing at Slick's school." She finally makes it to the counter to sit stuff down. "That's the last time he's allowed to go pick him up."

Kara rolls her eyes. "Tell me about it. My kids aren't even in school yet and he signed me up. He and I will be having a long talk about this before Krista starts school. He should know I'm not a baker." She places the baby in the small bassinet we have.

Chelsea waddles in and puts Harm in the pack-n-play. "I may go to jail for killing my brother-in-law," she says before sitting on one of the stools.

"How is Marco doing after hearing about his friend?" Sloan asks as she unpacks ingredients.

I shrug, "He's okay, I'm glad the boys were able to go with him. That makes me feel better."

I smile as I watch Sage get Krista and Linc settled with snacks and juice boxes in the den.

"Okay, ladies, what are we baking?" I ask, laughing.

Sloan sighs, "I decided brownies and chocolate chip cookies will be the easiest."

I smile and shrug, "Okay, let's get started." I start getting out my mixer and clearing off my island so we can spread out, while the girls get to work separating the supplies.

I wish my parents had gotten to meet all of these girls. They'd be so happy with who the boys ended up with and let's face it, my daddy would be over the moon that Vance and I finally 'got our heads out of our asses' and ended up together.

I could say I regret ever meeting Jeffery Storm and Vance ever breaking my heart, but I probably wouldn't have this right here and in the end that's all that matters.

CHAPTER 26

MARCO

Three Years Later...

We're having another charity event tonight and Roundman's daughter and son-in-law are visiting, I'm excited to check on them. It's been an eye-opening three years. Finding out that a great friend of mine died, well, it was a real kick to the gut. When I was young and met Roundman and Danza, I really had no clue where my life was going to go. I planned to retire from the Corps but when that didn't happen, they offered me a family and a place with the same brotherhood. My path, though, it led me back here to my hometown, the place I never wanted to be. Now, glancing around our house before Elaine and I head out for the arena, I can't help but feel nostalgic looking at the pictures. I do this a lot. There are ones dating back to Lainey and me in high school, to our years with the boys at the gym, their kids, all of our adopted family and even a few kids we've fostered over the years. So many memories, so many that I missed. Too much time that I missed all because we were young and stupid. However, in my heart I know that if we'd stayed together, I wouldn't have Liz, and we may not have Sly and Huck or any of the rest of our rag tag crew.

Elaine comes around the corner with her purse. "Are you ready to go, sweetie?"

I smile at her. "Yeah, babe."

Opening the door of my truck for her to get in, I smile. "Have I told you how happy I am that you're mine?" I ask.

She grins, "Not today, but I never get tired of hearing it."

The drive to the arena is short, and I'm excited to get there. This is the first event that I haven't taken any part of planning. Huck and the others have done an excellent job, I can already tell. It's taken a lot for me to let go. I still show up at the gym most days, especially on the days Lainey works. I still like to give Sly and Lox pointers when they fight and tonight will be the first time ever that I'm not working their corner. I'm here tonight completely as a spectator.

Since Lainey has finally figured out that I taught the boys not to get their asses handed to them, she's started coming a little more. Walking in through the back to avoid the crowd, I see our crazy family in one of the side rooms.

"So there I was up to my elbows in literal shit and all this fucker can do is laugh." Sly is explaining something I'm not sure I care to understand and pointing to Huck.

"Sly, the kids are in here," Elaine scolds. "How do you expect them not to have the mouths of sailors if you don't watch it?"

He comes over and kisses her on her head. "Sorry, Mom, I'll watch it. I was telling them about one of the times that my princess got sick when she was a baby and sh-pooped all over me."

Krista is fourteen now and from the look on her face she's thrilled with her dad telling this story. I'm fairly certain he's only telling it because Linc brought a friend with him tonight that is a year older than him, so he's her age and the two of them are making puppy eyes at each other.

Oh boy. When that girl starts dating, it's going to throw him into a tailspin.

I look over at Slick, damn, he's finishing up his Junior year in high school and is probably going to end up going to college on a football scholarship. That kid is amazing. I can't help but think back to that day he walked in the gym in his little wind suit and wife-beater, missing his two front teeth and telling the boys that he wanted to work out and get bigger muscles. He introduced himself like a damn mini adult, "I'm Sage Foster. Nice to meet you," as he shook hands with all three of the guys.

Huck gives a deep chuckle. "Nice grip you got there, Slick." And after that the kid had us.

One of the kids yells at the other one, bringing me away from my memories. Suddenly, the room feels like it's tilting a little so I take a seat. My blood pressure might be up a little, worrying about this event going off tonight without any hitches for the boys.

We talk with the guys for a little longer before we head out to our seats to watch the fights. The arena is alive with excitement. I'm proud of the boys, they've done well tonight. Lox's fight goes pretty quickly, so does Gibbs', Sly takes a little bit of a beating during his and last up is Sergio. I'm sitting at the edge of my seat, we're in round three and it's getting touchy. I can see his wife, Paige, flinch each time he gets hit. The bell rings and the round is done. There is a discussion by the judges and they finally declare Sergio the winner. I automatically look to the opponent's side and can see they're pissed off. It was a tough fight and I'm sure it was even tougher to judge. I turn to Lainey, "I'm going to go meet the boys in the locker room."

She laughs, "You've stayed to the side as long as you can, huh?"

I nod, laughing at her before I get up and head to the locker room. As I'm walking down the hallway I can already tell it's going to be one of those nights. I hear raised voices down the hall. "You motherfuckers think you run this damn circuit because you have some damn contract bullshit! Fuck you! I should've won that match."

I can hear Sergio trying to be reasonable. "Look, man, you know yourself that was a tough match-up and I'm sure it was a close call by the judges. Tonight was just for charity anyway."

"I don't need you patronizing me, motherfucker, I'll beat your ass right now." When I round the corner I see that the guy is up in Sergio's face, with his little crew.

Huck makes the move to get in front of his fighter like I taught him to and points to the exit. "You and your crew need to leave, this isn't the place for your bullshit."

The boy switches his attention to Huck. "I'll kick your ass, too, brah."

Huck cracks his neck. "I'm not your brah, but this is my event and my gym is the sponsor so get the fuck out."

"That's okay, I know you guys are pussies and that old man isn't around anymore to cover your asses for what fuck-ups you really are." This coming from the guy who is their trainer. Yeah, I've always hated that guy, he runs a sketchy crew.

Stepping forward, I clear my throat. "Ahem. The *old man* is still around, he just knows his fighters and partners don't need him to wipe their asses every time they take a shit. Now, do as Huck asked and get the fuck out of here." I turn to the fighter. "You're so sure you can take our guy, you call back up on Monday and schedule a real match, I'm sure he'd be happy to accept your offer."

They flip me off and make their way to the rear exit.

I walk over and hug all of the boys with back-slapping hugs. "I'm proud of what you guys did tonight. Come on to the house, bring all of the kids, Lainey and I smoked a couple of boston butts today and made a bunch of sides." Used to I would take all of them to eat but, this crew is getting too big to take to a restaurant.

They all nod and I head out to let all of their families know and so we can get going to the house.

A couple of hours later, they've all gotten to the house and eaten until they're about to pop. Lox hugs Lainey, "Thanks for feeding us, Mom, it was great."

All of a sudden my stomach feels queasy; I think I may have ate too much or the pork just isn't settling well. I make it to our bathroom and start sweating. Turning my head, I throw up in the toilet. A pain shoots down one of my arms and I know what's happening. I open the door and yell, "Lainey!"

She comes running down the hall followed by one of the boys. "Vance!" She turns back to the hall. "Call 9-1-1!"

Huck comes in, "Sit down, Marco."

I see Elaine shoving something in his hand, but I'm so dizzy I can't tell. "Here, put this aspirin in his mouth to chew up."

He does as he's told. "Stay with me, Marco, they're getting help. Chew this up."

Lox comes running down the hall. "The ambulance just pulled up outside."

Lainey takes my hand. "They're here, baby, we're gonna beat this."

I make it as far as the living room before I fall. I come to briefly as they're putting me in the ambulance, and again on the ride. The next time I come to is going into the hospital. I look up at Lainey, she's running the show somewhat and I just know I love her. I grab her hand and croak out, "I love you." Then a bunch of alarms start going off and she screams.

"No! Don't you do this to me, Vance DeMarco! Don't you leave me again!"

I watched her.

For too long I simply watched her.

I loved her.

I loved her more than anything.

I lost her.

Then I found her again.

I never planned to let her go, not ever.

That's the thing about life, though, it doesn't always go as planned. The woman I love is still the girl I loved from high school. Our journey to be together went on for over twenty years and our life together has been full of kids and grandkids.

If this is where it ends, then it's been one hell of a ride.

EPILOGUE

ELAINE

One Year Later...

Waking up in a bed by myself is something I don't think I'll ever get used to. I've officially retired from nursing, but I'm getting restless. I may need to go pick up a shift every now and then to keep me young. Hell, I'm only fifty, but after Vance's heart attack I couldn't handle the long hours anymore.

Pushing myself up out of the bed, I stretch and find my slides that I wear around the house. Making my way to the kitchen, I do a pod of coffee. No one drinks it now but me, so no sense in making a large pot, I just do one of the pods. Going to the stove, I make an egg-white omelet, with spinach and low-fat cheese.

My day feels mundane. The back door flies open and in barrels Krista and Sage arguing, which is what they seem to do here lately. "I told you, Sage, this is the dumbest idea you've ever had and you're going to live to regret it."

Harm and Selah follow them in the door, dragging up the rear. "Hey, Grandma," they both mumble.

I point to the two who just blew through. "What are they arguing about?"

Selah puts her hand on her hip. "Well, a couple of things. First, it started because Slick wouldn't let her drive over here when he came to pick us up." She talks with her hands and her facial expressions are just like her daddy. "Which he tried to tell her it's against the law because he's nineteen, not twenty-one. Then, she got a text from some guy that he hates and is mad because the guy is seventeen and she's just turned fifteen." She rolls her eyes. "That spiraled into him being an idiot for telling Carrie that they needed to take a break while she was gone for the college abroad program or whatever. Now, I think they're just arguing to argue. I don't know." She takes a deep breath finally. Never a dull moment with this kid.

Harm clears his throat. "Anyway, we came over to help you with chores today."

I ruffle his hair, he's a good mixture of his parents. "Well, thank you, it's always nice to have some extra hands around here."

I turn back to the stove, "Did you guys eat breakfast?"

He shakes his head. "No, Slick was supposed to stop, but I think he forgot with the yelling and all."

I just nod and start cooking. It's nice to have people to cook for as I break the last egg in the frying pan. I don't get to cook a big breakfast much anymore unless the whole crew comes over. I feel an arm go around my waist and stubble rub my neck. "I don't think that's on my diet, Nurse DeMarco."

I giggle because it tickles. "Well, it's not, Mr. DeMarco, yours is on the counter, but we were invaded by four grands who have come to help you on the farm today. I missed you when I woke up this morning."

"Mmm, sorry, had to check that mama cow. Do you think we can send them outside to get started and I'll catch up after we have some time alone in the bedroom?" Ever since his heart attack, one they called a widow maker, he's trying to live life even fuller than he already did. One of the biggest things is the man has gotten the libido of a man half his age. He wasn't lacking in the department to start with but, woohoo now.

I laugh, "I doubt it, I'm pretty sure that's why they're here. I know Linc was at a sleepover last night and Virginia stayed with the twins, so something tells me this help we got was so their parents could do the very same thing without prying ears."

He shakes his head and goes to grab my cup. "Nope, buddy, no coffee for you," I say, snatching my cup away. "You've got juice in the fridge."

"If I have to give up coffee I think you should, too."
We hear yelling and a door slam. "Do I want to know?" he
asks.

I shake my head, "No, but you may wanna go have
a chat with your eldest grandson before he pulls a stupid
stunt that you have experience with. If you don't, he's
gonna be miserable and Krista may kill him."

I laugh as he shakes his head, walking away.

MARCO-

Stepping out on the front porch of the house, I
breathe in the fresh air. After my heart attack I decided it
was time to really retire from the gym, they were doing
great on their own anyway. I left it to the boys and Liz, we
bought this small farm, I changed my diet and have been
living happily ever after with the love of my life. Seeing
Slick sitting on the front porch staring out at the cows, I
take a seat next to him. "So, you wanna tell me why you're
tearing the front door off the house and Krista is yelling
loud enough to wake the dead?"

He bites his lip. "Not really."

"Okay, well let's see, you're nineteen so what could
your big issue be? Your phone ran out of data or storage?"
He looks at me like I've lost it. "Your mom is still buying
you undies with superheroes on them?" The look continues
but he laughs at least and shakes his head. "You caught
your Uncle Sly and Aunt Kara again?"

His eyes bulge. "No! And you guys said you'd never bring it up again." He rolls his eyes, "I broke up with Carrie."

"Why in the world would you do a thing like that?" I ask, shaking my head.

He sighs. "She is doing that semester abroad thing and I feel like she needs some space while she does that. I'm playing football for UF, I'm having experiences, I feel like it's only right for her to have room to have them, too."

I throw my hands up. "Wait just a damn minute. Have you cheated on that girl with a damn jersey-chaser?" My voice comes out rough, I know, but she's a part of this messed up family, too.

"Ugh. No, Gramp, but she's gonna be gone and we're not just talking about one semester. She's talked about doing a couple. There are going to be girls all around me, I don't want to slip. I've talked to Lucas, he told me how hard it was when he was in college, how he loved Mom, but he should've let her go. That it's a lot of temptation. She's gonna be all over the world with guys from all over. She might slip, but I feel like she needs the space."

"First of all, you don't need to take damn advice from Lucas and if he had let her go earlier you wouldn't be here. Second, if you don't want to slip, you won't. Lucas may have helped make you, but Lox is your dad and I know he raised you. Third, I don't believe for a minute Carrie would cheat on you. You guys need to talk about this. Don't think you know what's best for her. That's one of the worst mistakes I ever made in my life. I was eighteen and thought I knew what your grandma needed and it took me almost twenty years to get it worked out. It was a lot of needless pain on both of our parts because I was selfish and made decisions for both of us." I stand up and put my hand on his shoulder. "You hear me?"

He nods. "Yes, sir."

"Come on, Grandma should have breakfast ready, then I need you to help me with the cows."

Once I'm in the kitchen I see the breakfast bar full of kids eating and my Lainey's face bright with a smile. That's one thing she's missed since we've moved out here, the kids being around all the time. I kiss her on the cheek and take my healthy breakfast and sit down with them, just about the time the back door opens again and the rest of our kids and grands flood in.

Who would've ever thought the boy from the trailer park could have a great life like this? But that woman standing in the kitchen…she made me.

ACKNOWLEDGMENTS

Thank you to my readers. Without you, I would not be having this awesome adventure. You have helped make my dreams come true and for that, I'm truly blessed and grateful. I never would've dreamed Lox would take off like it did and that people would love the rest of the characters just as much. Now, here we have come full circle.

To my family, thank you for being supportive and understanding about my time.

Thank you to my friend Erica for staying on top of me about this book when I needed it.

I need to give a big Thank You to Chelly Peeler. She's not only my editor but my friend. She always listens to my random crazy thoughts. She loves my characters and understands my craziness. Thank you again.

To my bestie, Chelsea Camaron, thank you for being my sounding board. Thank you for giving me those little bits of advice, for helping me think three books ahead. Not thinking my random late-night texts are crazy or annoying. Understanding my need to format as I go and not laughing too hard at my attempt to outline the rest of the series. Love you. #commentbubblinbitch #blurbbitch

Kimberley Foster Holm for treating my books like Where's Waldo and helping me find those little things that I've read over a hundred times. #warnagirl

Thanks to my PA Shawna Powell. I just don't know what I would do without you. You are always up for a challenge and I wouldn't have gotten this story done without you taking care of social media so I could write. XOXO Big hugs.

Thanks to all of the book bloggers out there who spend so much time helping us promote books and everyone who leaves a review, you are all awesome.

To my street team, Donaldson's Dirty Debutantes, and S.M. Donaldson's Reading Room, you guys are just awesome. I don't know what I would do without you.

To my author friends, thank you for being supportive and inspirational all at the same time.

ABOUT THE AUTHOR

S.M. Donaldson is a born and raised Southern girl. She grew up in a small rural town on Florida's Gulf Coast, the kind of place where everyone knows your business before you do, especially when your daddy is a cop and your mom works for the school system. She married one of her best friends at the age of 20 and has two sons. She is a proud military wife, has always had a soft spot for a good story, and is known to have a potty mouth. At the age of 31, she decided there was no time like the present to attempt her first book. Sam's Choice was born and she hasn't stopped since. If you are looking for a good, steamy, Southern set romance with true Southern dialect, she's your girl.

My Links:
www.smdonaldson.com
www.facebook.com/s.m.donaldson.author
www.goodreads.com/AuthorSMDonaldson
Twitter: @SMDonaldson1
Instagram: SMDONALDSON1981

Other Titles by S.M. Donaldson

(New Adult Title Box Sets)
The Sam STRENGTH Series
The Temptation Series
The Secrets of Savannah Series
Novellas
Just the Other Sister Series
(E-book only)
Seasons of Change Novella Series
Summer of Forgiveness
Falling for Autumn
Holiday with Holli
Camilla In Bloom

(Adult Titles)
Marco's MMA Boys
Lesson For Lox (Short Story)
Letting Lox In
In Sly's Eyes
Holding Huck's Heart
Gaining Gibbs
Crazy Christmas (Short Story on Insta Freebie)
Jacob Exposed
Sergio Spiraling (Novella)
Sergio's Redemption
Making Marco

Dispatch 247 (Marco's Spin-Off)
Arrested Heart

(Young Adult Titles)
Game Time Series
Crimson Catch
Guarded Heart
Play on the Field

Check out this excerpt from
Arrested Heart
Dispatch 247
Book 1
By: S.M. Donaldson

Copyright © 2017 SM Donaldson
Cover by: Indie Vention-Designs
Cover Model: Tyler Morris
Photography by: E.B. Photography
Editing by: Chelly Peeler

DESCRIPTION

Mox

Life has a way of throwing curve balls at every turn. I'm Eli "Mox" Moxen and I've finally figured out what I want in life.

I'm fearless. In life, in my career, and in love. I'll face it all with strength and determination.

Amber

Just when I think I'm getting ahead, something comes along to knock me on my butt. I'm Amber Young, single mom, jaded in love, and in danger.

I refuse to fail. For my daughter and for myself, I refuse to fail at life, in my career, and in love.

For first responders like Mox, there is rarely a second chance for anything...except maybe love. This is Mox's chance to show Amber he's a man who also refuses to fail...especially when it comes to her heart.

Rarely is there a second chance at anything for a first responder...except maybe love.

The Call

"Alachua 247 to Alachua 27, we have a signal 24 in progress at the Citizens Central Bank on Volusia Boulevard. Proceed with caution, suspects have hostages and suspects are said to be armed."

"Alachua 27 10-4 Alachua 247. I'll be 10-51, 10-52 five minutes."

"10-4 Alachua 27, Alachua 16, 32, 5 and 22 will meet you there."

"10-4."

Prologue-
Mox-

I jump up from the bed, grabbing my black BDU-style pants and grab my SWAT gear. I glance back at the naked girl lying in my bed. She smiles at me. "You've got to go, huh?"

"Yeah, so you should probably get dressed." I say as I toss the condom into the garbage can. God, I hate freaking condoms, but I don't really know this chick well enough to go without. Christy, isn't that her name? Christy, yeah, that seems right. Maybe Chelly? Cheryl? No, it's Christy I'm pretty sure.

She looks at me kind of sad. Shit, this happens every time I bring a girl back here more than once. From now on, I'm going to their damn place. "Look, you don't have to go home, but you can't stay here. My sister doesn't like me leaving my *guests* here when I leave."

Her eyes pop open wider. "Seriously?!" She jumps up from the bed, snatching her clothes on. "You're a real asshole. Blaming your sister, she seemed sweet the other day when I ran into her."

Shit, I gotta tell Gia not to talk to them. "She is nice, but only to a point." I'm dressed. "Now, I gotta go and so do you."

She grabs her bag as she goes out the door, "Fucking dick! Don't ever call me again!"

Yep, I sure won't. Because, I didn't plan to anyway. What in the hell does this chick expect? I've fucked her two times now. Both times, I ran into her at the coffee shop down the street after my night shift. Hell, this time I didn't even pay for her coffee. She basically followed me. I like sex, so sue me if a woman is willing to give it to me. I said no strings. I meant it. Oh well, it's not the first time I've been called names and it won't be the last.

Chapter 1
Mox-

"You think you're ready for this, rookie?" Mack asks me.

"You bet," I say as I strap on my Swat gear. Being the newest member to the team, my heart still thumps with excitement when I get a call like this one. It almost gets my dick hard. I mean it's the equivalent of prom night in high school where you're pretty sure you're going to get laid.

We've had a string of bank robberies going on throughout our county and the neighboring ones. They get in quick, thirty minutes after the bank opens, just enough time for all the vaults to be open and all the teller's drawers to be full. We've been close several times. Today is the first time they've gotten hemmed up in there. They're either getting brave or one of their crew fucked up.

Mack slaps me on the back and shakes his head, smiling. "Damn sure aren't that scrawny kid I met."

"Nope." I laugh as I tighten the strap on my tactical vest.

Yeah, I remember being that kid. I was eighteen when my twin sister Gia and I looked up our brothers. My self-confidence was in the tank, due to things beyond my control. I wasn't ever bullied or anything like that, but after my adoptive mother died, I just withdrew from life. My brothers Huck and Sly pulled me into their gym and started sparring and training with me. I needed that. I needed to be torn down and built back up stronger.

I was in college when Mack came in as a guest speaker for my State and Local Government class. When I spoke with him after class, he offered to take me on some ride-a-longs. That day, that one class changed my life.

I rode with Mack the entire time I was in college. He told me I needed to make sure I still got my degree, that way when I graduated from the Law Enforcement Academy and went to work, I wouldn't be stuck on patrol for forever before moving where I wanted to be. Now here I am, two years out of college, on our small SWAT team and working alongside Mack as an investigator. The youngest person to ever accomplish that in our department.

"Okay, they're about to come out!" our team leader announces.

The guys come out but only two of them, all the reports before said four guys. What the fuck? This makes no sense. No hostages, no hurry and they look terrified. But I guess if I had assault rifles pointed from every direction around me, I'd be scared, too.

"Drop your weapons, take three steps forward and get on your knees!"

The assailants drop to the ground, no issues. I look at Mack. "Not that I wanted a big shoot out or anything, but doesn't this seem a little off?"

He nods. "Yeah, something isn't right here."

He and I walk forward, taking the two suspects. The one I cuff is shaking and sweating, he's so nervous. He's whispering something. "What?" I question.

He whispers, trying not to move his lips. "We're a diversion. I'm a loan officer." I shove him into the patrol car and run back to Mack, just about the time the doors to the bank explode.

The concussion from the explosion rattles my ears and I'm thrown to the ground. I know I'm screaming even though it sounds muffled. "MACK!" I try to hold my eyes open, but it all goes black.

I wake up in a hospital room and I hear people mumbling. I try to speak but I have to clear my throat. My brothers and my sister are standing there. Gia is crying. They turn to me and start speaking but it's mumbles. I shake my head. "I can't hear you," I croak out.

Huck nods and grabs a notepad from the table and writes on it. "You were in an explosion."

I nod. "Where's Mack?"

He scribbles on the pad. "Getting patched up. He got some cuts and scrapes."

I point to myself. He scribbles again. "You're fine, your hearing is going to be rattled for a little bit, they said it's normal for an explosion. You'll be bruised up. You hit your head pretty hard on the pavement. Luckily there was no damage to the pavement," he jokes.

"Ha ha!" I say. "Gia," I croak. I motion to the pitcher sitting on the table.

She grabs a cup and fills it with water. I take a few sips. She grabs the pad from Huck. "You scared me to death."

"I know. Sorry," I say as I pull her in for a hug.

The doctor comes in a few minutes later to tell me I have to stay overnight due to hitting my head. Other than that, I should be able to go home in the morning and hopefully my hearing will return to normal in a few days. Until then, I'm off work. Which sucks.

~*~

A few days later, I'm going stir crazy in my apartment. My sister Gia is being a mother hen. She has her issues, but she means well. We found out a couple of years ago that she's bipolar, something she got from our birth mother. She almost turned our brother's entire gym upside down in the process, but we got her help. As long as she stays on her meds, she's fine, but she feels safer living with me. It doesn't bother me, normally I'm not here much. It means the fridge always has food when I come in, and my laundry stays caught up. Right now, though, I wish I was here by myself.

My hearing is almost back 100%, so I hear her trying to tell me what to do. "Gia, I love you, okay? But I'm a grown man."

"Eli, I'm just looking out for you. You don't have to be such a shit about it," she sasses, walking back into our small kitchen. She's pretty much the only person left that calls me Eli. After meeting Sly and Huck, Sly started calling me Mox, for my last name Moxen, and it just kind of stuck. To be honest, after all the changes I went through in college and meeting brothers we never knew about, I didn't feel like Eli anymore, but Mox did feel like it fit.

I gotta get out of here for a bit. Standing up, I grab my keys and wallet. "I'm going to the gym."

"Wait. No, you don't need to be driving. I'll take you."

"Gia, I'm fine. My hearing is back, I go back to work in three days. For that matter, deaf people do drive you know." I pull her into a hug. "I appreciate you wanting to take care of me, but I need to leave this apartment. Alone."

She smiles up at me. "Okay. Just be careful and don't let our brothers talk you into sparring."

I grin before walking out the door to my truck.

~*~

"So how did you get away from Florence Nightinghell?" My brother, Sly, jokes about Gia as we spar in the MMA gym he owns part of.

They all know she's kept me locked up since the explosion. "I just told her I had to go. I had to get the hell out of that apartment. She did tell me not to let you guys talk me into sparring, though."

Sly shoves me. "So that's the first thing you ask to do when you come in here. Jackass."

I hear a bunch of commotion in the room next door. "What are they doing in there today? Old ladies frisking your twin?" Huck sometimes teaches a Senior Citizens Self-Defense Class. To say an old lady or two has copped a feel is a complete understatement.

He laughs. "No, not today. Women's Kickboxing is in there now." He glances at his watch. "Should be getting out anytime."

"When did you guys start kickboxing classes?" I question as I swing at him again.

"Um, a few months ago. All our wives' idea. Something about getting off baby weight and kicking ass. I've learned not to question."

We go back to trying to hit each other when the classroom door opens and out walks about a dozen women. Several I'm basically related to, but one that looks as beautiful as she did at sixteen. I don't think she knows who I am, I never went out of my way back then to introduce myself. We had a couple of classes together since I was advanced, but she was a year older. Then she got pregnant and left school.

Chelsea comes running over to me, full-on speed and takes me down. "Shit, Chels. Get off of him," I hear her husband, Huck, say. "He was almost blown up a couple of days ago."

Chelsea pins me to the floor. "Yeah, about that. I'm not sure I like you being on the SWAT team now."

I continue to let her think I can't get out of her hold. "Chelsea, I'll be fine. The other day was something freak and you know it."

"Yeah, but I also know what else can happen." Chelsea's dad was on the force, he was shot when he and Mack arrived at a call about a bank robbery. She was working at the hospital at the time. It was a mess, I hate stressing her out.

"Chels, I promise to be more careful. Okay?"

She shoves me in the chest, climbing up off me. "Okay, but if you so much as break a nail, I'm calling Mack and telling him to take you off the squad."

I shake my head. "Okay. Whatever."

Sly's wife comes over and I excuse myself to the locker room to change. Walking down the hall, I wipe my face with the towel I placed around my neck, when a pile of red hair comes barreling out of the women's locker room, running straight into my chest. "Omph."

"Oops, sorry," the young girl says shyly.

I chuckle. "It's okay. Just watch where you are going, don't want you to get hurt."

"Carrie, come on!" I hear shouted behind me.

I turn around to see her, "She was coming, we accidentally bumped into each other. I was apologizing," I explain, not wanting the little ball of fire to get into trouble.

"Oh. Sorry." She walks down the hall to me. "I'm Amber. You look familiar, like I should know you, more than just from in here." She shakes her head "I just can't quite place it."

I nod. "We went to high school together."

"Oh." She blushes a little.

I wave her off, "Don't sweat it, I was about fifty pounds lighter and a year younger than you. We did have a few classes together, though." Shit, I sound like a damn love struck teen. "Anyway." I point to the locker room. "I need to get changed."

"Okay. Sorry again about her running into you." She turns and then snaps back. "Your name?"

"Huh?"

"You didn't say your name," she replies.

"Oh. Eli Moxen. Mox."

She smiles. "Well, it was good to see you, Eli. Come on, Carrie, I can't be late."

She turns, leaving me in the hallway and like an idiot I just stand there. I can't help but watch her ass as she walks away. I'd love to see that ass naked, preferably while driving into it from behind. She's that girl, the one from your past that you've always wondered about.

Fuck. I need a shower. A cold one.

www.ingramcontent.com/pod-product-compliance
Lightning Source LLC
Chambersburg PA
CBHW030327200626
46816CB00006BA/1953